I0655040

What Will Poor Robin Do?

Book 4 of the Kelly Murder Mysteries

A novel

Written by S. G. Lee

Copyright 2017 © Sheilagh G. Lee

First Edition 2017

SB

An imprint of Shillelagh Books

London, Ontario, Canada

This book is a work of fiction. Names, characters, places, any references to historical events and incidents are either products of the author's imagination or are used fictitiously. Any resemblance to actual events or locales or persons, living or dead, is entirely coincidental. All rights reserved. No part of this book may be used or reproduced in any form or by any electronic or mechanical means including information storage and retrieval systems, without written permission from the author. The only exception is by a reviewer, who may quote short excerpts in a review. All rights reserved including the right to reproduce this book in any form whatsoever

Acknowledgments:

Sincere thanks to Jodi and Sydney, without your constant support and encouragement, this book would not be possible. You are the best friends a writer could have. I dedicate this book to my daughters, my son-in law and my husband; who have supported my writing endeavours with encouragement and love. Special thanks to my beloved mother in heaven, who taught me dreams, can come true with hard work, perseverance and patience.

Copyright © 2017 by Sheilagh G.
Lee

All Rights Reserved

ISBN (13) 978-1987977226
(paperback)

ISBN-10: 198797722X

ISBN: 978-1987977219 (e-book)

Table of Contents

Chapter 1 - Bleak New Year's

Cold and raw the north wind doth blow,

Bleak in the morning early,

All the hills are covered with snow,

And winters now come fairly.

Wind doth blow and we shall have snow,

And what will poor robin do then, poor thing?

He'll sit in a barn and keep himself warm,

And hide his head under his wing, poor thing.

~Old Nursery Rhyme-Author Unknown

The day after Katha's wedding at the Airport

"Such a lovely wedding, you and

Grandpa Terrence looked so wonderful

yesterday. What a party! You danced into the night; while I watched you both twirl and boogie the night away. Grandpa Terrence can really dance. I think he put all of those younger guys to shame."

"He's really fit. The doctor says he's like someone twenty years younger," Katha answered.

"I think I had about three hours sleep," Lily stated.

"I told you to go up to bed, three times," protested Katha.

Katha then looked at the peaked Lily. Lily's face was drawn and worn looking and her hair hung limp and scraggily around her face.

"Are you sure you're okay?" Katha asked.

"I'm fine. I had my personal physician sit with me most of the night until I went up to my room," Lily laughed.

"Dafydd is pretty cute. Terrence is his godfather and says he was always a good kid."

"Yes, he is nice," Lily commented then a frown came over her face as she thought about how she met him and what Emmett had done.

"Do you want to talk about Emmett?" Katha asked.

"No! Can we change the subject?"

"You should see all the pictures I took," Amelia stated overhearing, "I'm taking them in so you can have a nice album of physical pictures, Aunt Katha."

"Physical pictures?" Katha asked.

"Adults over forty should come with manuals," Rose muttered under her breath then closed her eyes and went to sleep.

"I'll take the pictures off my phone and in the camera and transfer them to a disc; where I'll take them to a photo place and they'll develop them to pictures you can put in your album or on the wall," Amelia explained.

"That should make a nice album, along with the ones the photographer took," Katha cried, happily looking at the pictures on Amelia's camera.

"I'm glad you like them," Amelia said.

"Ooh, could I have a copy of this one? I'd like to blow it up and put it on our wall," Katha exclaimed.

"I can get that done at the photo place along with the others. What size do you want of you and Terrence dancing?"

"Oh that is a good one! You look younger than your years!" Lily commented looking over at the photo, she then yawned.

"I'd like an eight by ten," Katha stated.

Terrence then came back from the men's room and asked, "Eight by ten what?"

"Picture dear for our wall don't we look good in this picture?" Katha asked.

"We do," Terrence agreed.

"I'm going to take a nap until the flights called. Wake me up when our flight is called will you Grandma Katha?" Lily said.

"Me, too," Amelia said yawning.

"I will. Now go to sleep, my sweets," Katha answered then turning to Terrence she said, "A magical wedding, wasn't it, Terrence? A castle all my family and the man of my dreams; what more could a bride want?"

"I'm so glad that I married you Katha O'Malley," Terrence stated taking her in his arms and kissing her soundly on the mouth.

"That's Katha O'Malley- Stewart; thank you," Katha replied.

"Look at the children and they say youth has more energy. Rose and Carol are sound asleep, too," Terrence answered.

"They do look so sweet."

"It was a fun trip for them too despite the unpleasantness. Wasn't it?" Terrence enquired.

"Yes, darling, I think they had a good time, although something is up with Lily. I believe something more than breaking up happened to her and Emmett. She's not saying anything to me, though," Katha stated.

"Lily seemed fine to me. Are you sure?"

"Lily thinks she's hiding her hurt from me, but I see it. Something happened."

"Will you pry it out of Lily?"

"No, I'll wait and then get the whole story out of Amelia in about a week's time. Lily always confides in her cousin; or Lily will tell me in her own good time."

"You really love your girls. Are you sure they'll be okay if we take our week's honeymoon in Paris."

"What?"

Terrence showed Katha the airline tickets that said London Ontario to Toronto to Paris. Katha couldn't help it she squealed happily like a little girl, "We're going to Paris!!"

"Your girls are headed home to Happy Valley. I already told Lily and their flight leaves before ours."

"Oh, Terrence you spoil me. I haven't been to Paris since I was with... I'm sorry; I'm with you now I shouldn't bring up one of my other husbands," Katha stated.

"We both have a past, my darling girl. It's what's brought us to this true love. I understand you love Kieran, too. That's what made us what we are today the sums of our pasts, but I'm the lucky one I have you by my side. "

"No wonder I love you. You have a heart as big as an ocean."

"I have to if only to match you my darling, Katha."

Katha then glanced at the tickets again.

"Don't worry Grandma Katha. I booked the tickets and triple checked them. You're really going to Paris," Rose stated looking up at them with sleepy eyes.

"You're awake? Will you girls be okay if we go away?" asked Katha.

"We'll be fine, Grandma Katha. Rose, Carol, Amelia, and I will see you two when you get home; until then have fun," Lily exclaimed opening an eye and commenting.

"You included me as one of Grandma Katha's girls?" Carol puzzled.

"Why wouldn't I? You were always unofficial family before but now you're now officially family."

"Thanks, Mrs. Brooksfield," Carol answered her voice choking up.

"I'm your Aunt Lily now."

"Thanks, Aunt Lily. I'm tired too, somebody wake me up when they call our flight to Happy Valley," Carol said.

~0~

Francine and Gerald Banks

Francine glanced over at Gerald with

love. They had both celebrated this New Year's Eve; Gerald a little more than Francine. He'd given up the keys willingly; smiling that smile that melted her knees. Gerald looked over at Francine and smiled a goofy smile and Francine felt deliriously happy. She wanted to shout to the world that she and Gerald had reconciled.

Her girlfriends had told her she had lost her mind for forgiving and forgetting his indiscretions which had caused their break-up, but Francine had loved Gerald since she was a teen and that had never gone away. She needed him in her life and by her side.

Francine covered a yawn with her hand. Her head ached and she was tired; a little sugar would pick her up; one of those orange custard squares Daddy had given her would taste great right now. A little pick me up to get them home at four a.m. on New Year's Eve. Francine smiled again at Gerald and he touched her arm.

"I love you Francine, you are the best thing, which ever happened to me," Gerald claimed "I'll never cheat on you again."

"You'd better not. Or you can bet I'll take you to the cleaners with that pre-nup my lawyer drew up. I hope that's not just the champagne talking."

"It isn't. I promise we'll be a family again and Carol will be happy. You'll be happy too. I will really try harder this time, Francine."

"Just don't hurt us again, Gerald."

"Here, I'll prove my love to you. You were thinking about those lemon squares your Dad gave us; weren't you? Sometimes I think you love sweets, more than me."

"You do know me, and I love you more than life itself, Gerald," laughed Francine as Gerald held a square up to her mouth, eating another square himself with his other hand.

Francine made short work of the square not even tasting it, she ate it so fast. Coconut fell into her lap and with one hand she brushed it off taking her eyes off the road for a moment.

"Oh no Gera....aa...ld it has ginger in it!" cried Francine.

Francine grabbed her throat with one hand and tried to pull over before she passed out. Gerald tried to take the wheel, but in his excitement, the square he ate choked him and he seized his throat with frantic motions.

Francine passed out, her breathing laboured and then almost non-existent, Gerald too, his breath laboured as he can't even eke out a cough and tries to reach again for the wheel. Their car skidded into the path of a tractor trailer. The car, a mass of twisted metal hit a guard rail. It wound between trees and through grass and down an embankment.

Gerald choked up the square too late and died. Francine stirred for a moment between life and death and prayed, silently, "Dear Lord, I accept that it is my time; but please grant me one last goodbye to my daughter and find someone that will care for her as I would."

~0~

Carol

Carol snuggled deeper into the airport

chair hearing Terrence and Katha talk some more she stopped listening. She'd sleep until their flight was called. Three a.m. was an ungodly time to get up. It felt like she'd been up for eight hours and it was only nine a.m. Carol closed her eyes surrendering to the deep REM cycle of sleep, something however interrupted this. Carol felt herself stirring to a wakeful state and then felt her mother's hand touch her brow. Carol then struggled to open her eyes.

"Carol, honey wake up." Francine begged.

"Mom, I don't want to get up. I'm tired I want to sleep."

"Baby, please listen I don't have much time. I want to tell you how much I love you."

"Love you too, mom. Want to sleep now!" cried Carol keeping her eyes closely closed.

"Your dad and I both love you and we were together when we died," Francine began.

"What do you mean you died? I don't understand Mom? I think I want to wake up now. This dream is weird!" Carol cried opening her eyes.

Carol looked at her mother and saw that a mist surrounded her and there was a see through quality to her. What a strange dream.

"Why do you look like that?" Carol asked puzzled.

"It's a long story Carol and time is short. I want you to listen to me now, baby girl. You were the best thing in my life in besides your Dad. Being your mother? Truly a gift and a blessing; remember that!"

"I don't understand Mother .Why do you tell me this?"

"There's no easy way to say this, Carol. I'm dead baby! I'm so sorry to leave you. I choked on ginger and the car crashed. Your father and I are dead. I know you are terrified. This will be a trial for you my little love, but don't you will survive this. Rose will be by your side and she understands. Go to Rose, share with her and let her in. Your Grandpa Terrence will take care of you it's in our will."

Carol watched as Francine turned around quickly as a bright shiny light appeared. An outstretched hand reached for Francine pulling her close. Carol realized she knew that hand-it was Grandpa Crimshaw. Were they all dead? Mom said that she and Dad were dead. If Grandpa Crimshaw was dead too, how did he die? She wanted to wake up, now!!Then all this would go away but as she came fully awake and saw the airport again she could shake the feeling that nothing would change. This wasn't a dream at all; but a goodbye. It had to be… it had seemed so real. No, she was borrowing trouble as Grandma Katha said. Wasn't she?

Carol felt the tears coming down her face.
She questioned the dreams purpose for a few
seconds, trying to convince herself again
that it was a dream; some convoluted dream
conjured from her overtired mind.

However it felt real; not like a dream but
like an interactive video recording. She
looked around the airport as if she could see
their manifestations. Grandpa had been
mean and miserly. If he had died she should
feel some grief for his passing; but all she
could think was why he couldn't have just
died and her mother and father live.

Carol looked around begging for someone to
tell her the dream wasn't a premonition, or
her mother hadn't really appeared to Carol
after death. Carol felt numb inside; like
someone had turned on air conditioning in
the airport, an impossibility in winter. Now
she knew what they meant when they said
chilled to the bone. Carol looked over at
Rose slumbering on. Rose must have felt

this way when her father died and yet Carol hadn't really understood.

Carol felt bad; but she didn't feel this pain down to her very marrow, not about Rose's dad.

Carol heard her cell phone ring and ignored it. Looking to the caller she saw it was Great-Uncle Edward she didn't want to answer. She knew what he would say. She didn't want to hear it, if no one said it, it wasn't true!

"Well, hello, Edward," Terrence answered as his phone rang seconds later, "I'm sorry you weren't able to get away for our wedding. It was wonderful everyone had fun. ...What? Say that again... No, that can't be possible! That can't be true."

Terrence face appeared ashen and in that moment he looked like he had aged twenty years.

"Terrence, what has happened? Tell me!"
Katha demanded, worried.

Terrence couldn't seem to form words; so
Carol took a big breath and said calmly,
"My Mom and Dad are dead and so is my
Grandfather Crimshaw."

Terrence didn't dispute what Carol said,
tears coming from Carol's eyes.

"How do you know that Carol? Are you
psychic?" asked Rose.

"My mom told me," Carol answered.

"But if your mom is dead how could
she....?"

Lily stared at Rose hard and then Rose
exclaimed, "Carol, I can't believe this. I am
so sorry. Whatever you need I'm here."

"I'm so sorry, my darling grandchild. I
loved Francine with all my heart. I'd like to
believe my granddaughter did come to you
in your hour of need. We are all here for

you, Carol," Terrence said sadly wiping away tears.

"That's right, we'll cancel our honeymoon. You come first," Katha volunteered.

Terrence nodded and said, "Excuse me, a moment. I have to change our tickets to Happy Valley."

Terrence then went directly to the counter to change the tickets.

"This is real?" Carol asked, then resigned she sighed and said, "Yes, of course it is. I wanted it to be a horrible nightmare but it's awaking one. "

"Carol; I'm so sorry. Remember you have your family and we are with you now," Terrence said.

"Terrence is right. You are our great-granddaughter and we all love you. We are here for you, always," Katha stated.

"We love you, Carol. We are your family and here for you," Amelia stated.

"Come here, Carol," Lily insisted, as she wrapped her in her arms, "Amelia's correct; we are your family, Carol. Don't forget that. We grieve with you. I am so dreadfully sorry about your mother. I know how much it hurts to lose your mother; but each individual is different and I would never compare myself to you. I also understand that your pain is your own; but if you ever want to talk about anything I'm here for you."

"Thank-you all, I just want to think about them right now. It just seems so unreal, like I'm in a mist," Carol admitted.

"It will get better dear. I know it doesn't seem so; but it will," Katha advised.

"It will never be better," Carol answered then began crying.

Lily held onto Carol tight and let her cry; soon Carol wiped her tears and sat stoically waiting for the flight. Others in the airport looked on in sympathy and that made Carol feel even worse. She soon dried her tears when their flight was called. The staff, solicitous allowed them to board first.

Terrence, Katha, Amelia, Lily, Carol and
Rose all board the plane with heavy hearts.
They all thought of Carol as the plane took
off and they flew home.

Terrence stared to wonder if Francine
suffered. The Kelly ladies wonder if the
curse of the Kelly's had touched Terrence
and Carol's family and if this is the price
people paid for loving them.

The plane landed and they find the press
waiting for them shouting questions at them,
"Do you know anyone who would want to
murder your family members?" and "Is there
any connection to the murder of the mayor
months ago?" followed by "Is your family
cursed?"

Terrence steered them through stating, *"No
comment."* to the press. Terrence then
hustled them out of the airport to Katha and
Terrence's home. They were home, time to
face the music. The honeymoon was over
before it began.

~0~

Happy Valley

D ing dong, the asshole's dead. He

lorded over everyone. People thought
Harold Crimshaw had won fairly over Katha
O'Malley; but they were mistaken. Harold
Crimshaw had rigged the election in his
favour. He deserved to die; there was no
doubt about it. Not that Katha O' Malley
would have been a better mayor; but at least
she was honest.

Harold Crimshaw was evil incarnate. If no
one would do anything about such man well
then I had to do something. I couldn't allow
him to continue to use his position and
power to harm anyone else. Harold nattered
on about how you should go do what you
loved best while destroying lives. So
inspiration struck me. Harold loved oranges,
so oranges should kill Harold with a little
help from ginger. So me, the murderer (tee-
hee-hee, love that term murderer.) took his
life with what he loved most oranges.

Filling his ample gut with the sweet squares
I made with my own two hands. It was
really too bad that his daughter and son-in-
law were killed; but they really shouldn't
have been so greedy. The squares were
made so lovingly for Harold. His daughter
was his spawn so she probably had those
evil genes anyway and as for the son-in law
he could have been picked by Harold. I'd
heard he was a cheat and a terrible father. So
no great loss and yet I felt a measure of
guilt.

It wasn't my fault they ate them and that she
had inherited Harold's unusual allergy. I
mean really who's allergic to ginger? Harold
that's who! Except now he wasn't allergic to
anything anymore; except maybe the cold
hard ground.

I still had to dispose of the evidence. It must
not get in the hands of the police. The
evidence would implicate me. If they found
the squares...I must get the container the
squares were in. I must get there to Harold's

house and get access, but how? Where there's a will; there's a way. I knew of a way and I would take it. Harold was dead and he wouldn't harm anyone again and that was the way it would to stay. I would see to that.

The police really weren't looking at this as a crime. They think it was death by misadventure. Ha, ha, they think it's an allergy gone wrong. No crime involved; maybe I'm in the clear?

Barbara Franks was in charge at the Crown Attorney's office. Lily Kelly Wentworth-Brooksfield had stuck her nose in the wrong place on holiday and now was on sick leave. Something about her heart? You stick your heart in the wrong place and it get twisted Lily should have learned that a long time ago.

Timing was everything; Lily Kelly-Wentworth-Brooksfield was such a nosy broad. She wouldn't have let this go and then I would have had to do something to her.

Lily was such a lovely person too; so that would have really hurt to have to take action against her. She was even sweet to Barbara when Barbara was suffering her depression so bad that she lashed out at Lily. It really helped that Barbara was a stickler for the book; everything by the book no deviations. Barbara would close the case in no time. Despite the fact that when I committed this crime I didn't know the police chief Edward Stewart was related to that idiot Harold it wouldn't harm me. It wouldn't bring me down. I allowed myself a sigh of relief. Then I analyzed the problem. It wasn't my fault his stupid granddaughter ate what was meant for Harold and ended up killing herself and her husband. I mean really could I have predicted that? Should I have?

Edward Stewart was no fool. I must not underestimate him and his zeal to find me. The silly man wouldn't shut up about how someone had killed his great-niece. Funny thing, he wasn't complaining that much about Harold. I guess he didn't like him much either. Too bad, about the kid though, being an orphan was a tough gig. I feel bad about Carol Banks.

No kid should lose their parents so young, but then again it really wasn't my fault her mother was so greedy and killed them both and she was better off without her stupid cheating low-life father.

My plan was in action I had rid the world of a dirty politician, a pervert of the worst kind, a thug. So why was I feeling guilty? He chose his death not me!!

He had the choice to eat, or not eat the orange squares and he had chosen. I mustn't lose my focus I had to keep an eye on the investigation discreetly. No one must guess I was behind this. Blame got me nowhere. I must protect myself at all costs.

Barbara Franks was in charge at the Crown Attorney's office. Lily Kelly Wentworth-Brooksfield had stuck her nose in the wrong place on holiday and now was on sick leave. Something about her heart? You stick your heart in the wrong place and you get it twisted. Lily should have learned that a long time ago.

Timing was everything; Lily Kelly-Wentworth-Brooksfield was such a nosy broad. She wouldn't have let this go and then I would have had to do something to her. Lily was such a lovely person too; so that would have really hurt to have to take action against her. She was even sweet to Barbara when Barbara was suffering her depression so bad that she lashed out at Lily. It really helped that Barbara was a stickler for the book, everything by the book no deviations.

Barbara would close the case in no time; despite the fact that when I committed this crime I didn't know the police chief Edward Stewart was related to that idiot Harold. That wouldn't bring me down. I allowed myself a sigh of relief. Then I analyzed the problem. It wasn't my fault his stupid granddaughter ate what was meant for Harold and ended up killing herself and her husband. I mean really could I have predicted that? Should I have?

Edward Stewart was no fool. I must not underestimate him and his zeal to find me. The silly man wouldn't shut up about how someone had killed his great-niece. Funny thing, he wasn't complaining that much about Harold. I guess he didn't like him much either. Too bad, about the kid though, being an orphan was a tough gig. I feel bad about Carol Banks. No kid should lose their parents so young, but then again it really wasn't my fault her mother was so greedy and killed them both and she was better off without her stupid cheating low-life father.

My plan was in action I had rid the world of a dirty politician, a pervert of the worst kind, a thug. So why was I feeling guilty? He chose his death not me. He had the choice to eat, or not eat the orange squares and he had chosen. I mustn't lose my focus I had to keep an eye on the investigation discreetly no one must guess I was behind this. Blame got me nowhere. I must protect myself at all costs. Barbara Franks was helping me and didn't even know it. Soon she'd close the case and that would be the end of it. It would all be over. Wouldn't it? Of course, it would.

They'd never find me. I would always be that illusive murderer that none of them knew about. Too delicious!! I was a success at last. Take that daddy!!

~0~

Chapter 2 - Family

A few days after the funerals of

Francine, Gerald and Harold, with her heart still breaking for Carol, Lily walked in through the door of her home. She put away her coat and boots and walked into the kitchen.

"Don't you have class this morning?" Lily asked.

"I'm not skipping school there are parent/teacher interviews today. Remember? I brought home the notice to you," Rose answered.

"Oh, dear, I forgot to go. Your teachers must think me a terrible irresponsible parent," Lily said.

"Don't worry Lily, I subbed for you. Rose is doing very well in all her subjects. They actually would like her to take an advanced course at the university. I said would have to discuss it with you," Grandma Katha stated.

"A course at the university? Wow! What in?" Lily answered.

"Advanced maths. It's not a big deal," Rose answered.

"Sure it is. Not everyone is invited to take an advanced course at your age," Katha answered.

"Grandma Katha is correct; it is an honour. Be proud," Lily enthused, "I know I am so proud of you."

"Thank you mom, but my minds on Carol. I'm really worried about her," Rose said.

"Why? I know her parents died but she seems to be handling it well," Lily answered.

"A lot you know. Carol hides it well, but she's scared. She barely talks to me and she isn't even talking to Daria. Not that I should care about that but she always talks to her cousin."

"She's going through a lot give her some time," Lily insisted.

"Her parents are dead and some members of her family are fighting over her custody. She doesn't have time. Carol doesn't want to live with any of them. They're not there for her. You know they only want her money. You have to do something, mom. Carol's miserable."

"I wish we could adopt her, but her family would never allow that. Terrence's children think I'm the devil incarnate and that I brought bad luck to my husbands and now their family. Your grandfather Terrence is trying his hardest to get custody; but they are being difficult to say the least," Lily stated.

"Terrence's kids tolerate me; but I know they think I'm a jinx too, that will bring their father to ruin. But the goodness is Terrence and I have hired the best lawyer we could buy," Katha answered.

"Grandpa Terrence is too old and they'll use that against him, Grandma Katha. I know you hate that word, but the truth is you're old," Rose blurted.

"Rose...,"Lily admonished.

"She has to know the truth, mom. I looked it up in your law books; they don't like to award custody to old people, when younger people want to adopt relatives."

"I don't know what you expect me to do. I can't wave a magic wand and fix this Rose," Lily protested.

"Nor can I. But I'm trying Rose," Katha said sounding hurt.

"I don't know why I expected you to help. You can't even fix your own screwed up life. You broke up with Emmett and we don't see him anymore."

"Rose there are things about that you don't know," Lily protested.

"Rose Brooksfield…,"admonished Katha before she was cut-off.

"That's because you don't tell me. You just mope around here and make me worry. I think I hate you! You're so self-absorbed mom; all you think about is yourself!! I'm going to my room," Rose said stamping her feet and running to her room.

Lily looked at Rose with amazement. How had her daughter turned into this?

"Does she really believe all of this is my fault?" asked Lily hurt and dismayed.

"Teenagers, such drama queens! Don't worry about it; Rose will get over her temper tantrum and apologise to you. But you may have to update us all on the Emmett situation it's time dear you can't keep it all to yourself. We care about you. Now as for Carol we're doing the best we can. Terrence will get his children to come to an agreement soon. As much as they argue with him they adore him and some of them are afraid he'll leave his vast fortune to me should he die. Little do they know that I get a lump sum of one million and all his other millions go to them, except of course for his charity bequests...enough of this morbid talk I'll be around for a long time and so will Terrence."

"I know you will. I just don't want anything to happen to you," Lily responded.

"Nothing will happen to us; Quit borrowing trouble my dear. Right now were dealing with a lot of grief and guilt but it will get better over time. Poor Terrence is all torn up about this Barbara's superiors wanting to close the case and call it death by misadventure. It's a travesty!"

"Barbara is so difficult to deal with. I wish I could handle this for you," Lily exclaimed.

"I know you do, dear, Barbara says she has no choice but to do what her superiors' says. Terrence's son, Neddy is angrier than Terrence and he says that the Crown attorney, Barbara what's-her-face shouldn't be dictating to him how to do his job."

Lily laughed at this thinking what Barbara would say if she knew the police chief called her Barbara what's her face.

"Wait it gets worse Lily, don't laugh. Barbara acts like it's their entire fault they ate ginger by mistake and then hinted maybe Neddy should be happy they're dropping it. Then she insinuated that maybe someone in the family committed the crime or that Neddy committed the murders. I know Neddy hated Harold but he loved his niece.

He could never have hurt armed anyone, let alone a family member."

"Barbara is only trying to her job; even if she ruffles feathers easily," Lily protested.

"I never said Barbara wasn't doing her job; she just rubs me the wrong way. You know someone had to have made the orange squares and gave them to Harold. It wasn't an accident. He told everyone he was allergic to ginger. Someone knew that and used it against him and in the process they killed Carol's parents as well," Katha exclaimed, rapidly not allowing Lily to get a word in edgewise.

"I agree with you. Someone murdered all of them."

"I wish Barbara saw it that way. I really hate that woman. She is only concerned with her own position and how it looks to others."

"I know I worry she's after my job. Now that I'm sideline, she's really fired up to show she's the best Crown attorney."

"She can't make anyone believe she should have your job. You have not only the stamina to do the job correctly, but you also have charisma and common sense that helps you do the job better than Barbara. Don't worry people see through her. Now how did it go at the doctors? Did he say you can go back to work?"

"I have to admit Barbara is a tough prosecutor; but a little single minded when it comes to cases."

"Don't dodge my questions about the doctor. What did he say?"

"I have to have surgery again. Dr. Terrell said something about a flap not working correctly in my heart, due to the damage from the bullet," Lily stated quietly.

"You have to have surgery on your heart? That's pretty serious, Lily." Katha replied, "I'm sorry I was rambling on about Barbara. I'm sure it will all work out, dear. You should be concentrating on your health not problems like this."

"Believe me I need the distraction," Lily commented.

"Don't stress about Barbara. I'm sure it will turn out fine," Katha backtracked.

"I know that Barbara is a terrible stickler for doing it all by the books, but maybe I can talk to her about the investigation. I don't know how she can think of closing the investigation before it's even begun, Even if her superiors are demanding that she could speed it up," Lily answered.

"I thought so too but as I said she seems to worry only about her position. The police chief (Terrence's Neddy) ordered them to still investigate. It's very odd that Harold's Epi-Pen was missing. Harold always had one on him or at least close by and so did Francine. But it was New Year's Eve and possibly Francine didn't think she need it; after all her father always had his. Francine didn't even bring a purse. She probably thought she could use her Dad's Epi-Pen in a pinch."

"That is odd. I'll speak to Barbara about continuing her work into this; but I give no promises about Barbara's participation, Grandma Katha," Lily answered.

"Are you sure you should worry about this dear. I mean maybe you should be resting instead? When does your surgery take place?" asked Katha.

"Friday is the day Dr. Terrell scheduled my surgery. He says it needs to be done as soon as possible and no, I'm not okay with this. They are going to do surgery on my heart; all because a selfish woman who also decided she wanted my boyfriend didn't tell all she knew and got me shot," Lily cried.

"I hate that woman; but I feel sorry for the boy. Now it will be okay Lillypad. Dr. Terrell is working with Doctor Abrahams, correct? I've never met the man he's a relatively new hire to the hospital but he has great credentials. Doctor Abrahams is a trauma specialist. He knows what he is doing. He's probably done hundreds of these procedures," Katha insisted.

"I know it's just so scary. They're working on my heart. What am I going to tell Rose?"

"Just tell her you have to have a minor corrective surgery and that everything will be okay."

"I don't like lying to her. Grandma Katha."

"This is a minor fib that will protect the child. She's been through too much this year. She does need to be scared again."

"I guess you're right. Will you look after Rose for me?" Lily asked.

"Sure what is one more teen?" Katha enquired, and then Katha narrowed her eyes and said, "Wait a minute, you're not talking about permanently are you? Because everything will be fine! Now do you want to talk about that rapscallion Emmett Rogers and what he did to make you hate him, yet?"

"I guess so though it's embarrassing."

"Embarassing? I bet it's he who should be embarassed!! He made you unhappy and for that I'm mad at him!"

"Thanks it's good to know you're on my side, since you two are friends."

"His not my friend anymore you come first. Quit stalling out with it."

"I came to the room to accept his proposal. I was excited and oh so happy. I opened the door and there they were. Sherry-Anne was naked, her breast sticking out from under the sheet on his chest and he was naked too."

"That bastard."

"Grandma Katha, I've never heard you use such language."

"I've never had occasion to. Of all the evil things to do to you! I think she's behind it. How could that boy, not see that she was a piranha in heat? How could he propose to you and sleep with her? It doesn't add up, even with his boy in the mix."

"He slept with her. I was just the pale substitute for Sherry-Anne. You saw how much we looked alike, enough so someone shot me mistaking me for her."

"No one would willingly choose Sherry-Anne over you; I still think there's funny business there. That boy has rocks for brain and one day soon he's going to be sorry about his choices and then it will be too late."

"It's already too late. I'd never take him back after seeing them together. It was so devastating. I thought he loved me that I finally found a man I could trust."

"I'm sorry that he hurt you so, Lily."

"Me, too, but I'll get over it."

"Oh dear is that the time?" Katha said looking at her watch. I'm supposed to meet Terrence. We have to go to the reading of the will today. I believe it will prove that Terrence and I were named Carol's guardians. That should settle this court case and give us custody once and for all."

"Are you going to be okay with this? It's a huge responsibility," Lily asked, worried.

"I thought I didn't have it in me to raise another teen, but God has given me this challenge and I'll find the energy. I love that child like she's my flesh and blood and now that I married Terrence, she is.

"Even if she wasn't I've seen so much of that girl over the years, it's like she already was family," Katha stated.

"Carol's lucky. She has you; just like I did when I was young."

"You were lucky, only when you were young?" Katha replied sounding hurt.

"No, Grandma Katha, I'm one of the luckiest women in the world because I have you...always, in my corner and always helping and loving me," Lily amended.

"Well then, that's more like it!" sniffed Katha, "I'm thinking that you young lady should go up and have a rest so you can... what's the word those young ones use today... chill out? You go have a rest and when you get up, if you have a little time, and then you can talk to Barbara Franks about the case. Now scoot because I have to head out."

"Yes, Grandma Katha," Lily said, meekly going up the stairs.

Rose was sorry she'd been so mean to her mother and had wanted to apologise at least that was before she decided to listen in at the top of the stairs. Rose scurried to hide, so Lily didn't know she'd been listening in. Poor mom first Emmett cheats on her then she finds out she has to have surgery on her heart.

Rose had been an absolute beeyotch to her mother. What kind of a daughter was she being to Lily? Lily had taken her in and become the mother she needed and how had Rose rewarded her by yelling at her. She wanted to go apologise immediately but that would let mom know she heard everything and that would stress mom out more. Rose decided to quickly enter her room and shut the door quietly just before Lily came up the stairs.

Mom must not know she knew about the surgery that would only make it harder for her mother. She'd be a grown-up just this once and make things easier for Lily, the way Lily had always looked after her. She'd be the daughter Lily deserved not the trial she always been.

Life had gone to hell in this past year and it didn't look like it would get better any time soon. She finally decided to accept Emmett as her new step-father and he pulls a boneheaded move like this? Then Rose had the nerve to blame Lily for the break-up without any of the facts. How could she have hurt her mom this way? How could Emmett have hurt her mother this way? Sherry-Anne Mobley wasn't half the woman Lily was. Mom was kind and did nice things for people without expectation, unlike Sherry-Anne. She hadn't liked that woman since she met her. Rose had tried to be nice to her for Caleb and Emmett's sake, but now she wouldn't pretend anymore. If the woman came near her she walk the other way or ignore her all together Rose thought.

Rose had tried not being friendly with
Caleb, who was now attending her high
school, but it was like being mean to a
puppy and she couldn't do it. She was mad
at his parents, not Caleb. It wasn't his fault
his parents were idiots. Besides it was hard
starting at a new school in grade eleven in
the middle of the year. Caleb had no friends
except her and Carol. She didn't have the
heart to make that no friends at all at his new
school and it didn't hurt that other kids in
the school mistakenly thought that Rose and
Caleb were dating. This kept those other
guys from bothering her the way they did
last year simply because they were afraid of
Rose's boyfriend and other girls were
envious because he was so good looking.
Sometimes Rose wished he was her
boyfriend, he was a kind and gentle boy but
he seemed to look on her as a sister or a
friend.

Now mom cried every night when she
thought Rose was asleep. Lily had a broken
heart, not just because of that bullet that
Sherry-Anne Mobley had caused by taunting
the killer; but because that evil woman had
taken Emmett from mom as well. Rose
wished all kinds of ill luck and karma on

Sherry-Anne Mobley, even if she was Caleb's mother. The woman deserved payback for all the pain she'd caused Lily. Now she wished the woman would die. Well okay not die, that wouldn't be nice; but pain and sorrow wouldn't be too good for Sherry-Anne Mobley.

Rose was scared now. She had heard Lily mention heart surgery. People died from heart surgeries. She couldn't lose her mom. Why had she been so mean to her about Carol? It wasn't Lily's fault that Carol's relatives were infighting. Some of the relatives were reasonable and didn't care about the millions left to Carol by her parents, but some of them thought that custody would grant them access. They should just respect Carol's parent's wishes and let Carol be with Grandma Katha. Carol would be over her most of the time anyway. Didn't they realize that? Or maybe that was the problem? They thought that the Kelly's were cursed and that if Carol came to leave with Grandma Katha and Grandpa Terrence she'd fall under it too? Maybe they were worried about Grandpa Terrence as well?

They needed worry Grandpa Terrence was happy and so was Grandma Katha. Now if the grownups would get it together they'd settle Carol in her room at Grandma Katha's and all would be all right again.

~0~

Chapter 3 – Reading of the Will

Katha, Carol and Terrence entered the

offices of Brackenridge and Thorpe Law and Katha sighed. This wouldn't be an easy fix to Carol's problem, but surely the will of Francine and Gerald would state what Francine had always told them that should anything happened she'd designated Terrence and Katha as Carol's guardian.

A young woman an assistant to Carl Brackenridge gestured them into Carl's office where Katha noted saw another woman sat. The woman's bird-like figure sat ramrod straight in the chair. Her red hair pulled tightly into a bun, her eyes framed by horned rim glasses. She wore a business suit in grey with a white high collared blouse. Katha smiled at her and she offered a frown back. Who was this Katha wondered? Then she realized this woman must be Audrey as she already met Regan, (Neddy's wife) and Regan was sitting beside her husband.

Edward Stewart, (Neddy as his father called him) sat in a gray Brooks Brothers suit, his red hair thinning and some patches of his hair now gray, sat perched at the front of the chair looking like he'd leave at any moment. His wife, Regan, a Rubenesque woman almost as tall as him patted his hand and smiled reassuringly at him. Katha thought how truly beautiful that smile made Regan. They were a happy couple.

"Hello, Audrey. I'm so glad to finally meet you!" Katha cried as they walked passed Audrey to get to their seats.

"I'm sorry we couldn't make it to the wedding to welcome you properly into the family," Regan offered and elbowed Audrey as if to say don't be rude.

Audrey leaned over as if she'd say
something and Katha then reached out to
hug her; but Audrey ignored her comment
and shied away from the hug with a look of
disgust on her face. She then reached out
and hugged Carol who grimaced.

"Daddy, I'm so glad to see you," the woman
said leaping past Katha to embrace
Terrence.

"You didn't call. I didn't know you were in
town," rebuked Terrence.

"I just got in this morning. It's been a
whirlwind trip to get here, let me tell you."

Another woman interrupted the conversation
as she entered the room all dressed in black.
A young woman dressed in scrubs held the
frail woman's arms and guided her in.
Cecilia's short brown hair framed her face
and she stood about five two. She is trim and
is wearing a navy blue jacket and a long
navy blue skirt. She appeared to be young
possibly in her early fifties which would
make her younger than Edward; but several
years older than Audrey.

How young she was to have granddaughter
Carol's age, but Terrence had told Katha
that Cecilia had her daughter when she was
eighteen and Carol's mother had gotten
pregnant at fifteen years old with Carol.

Not that Katha had any right to talk she'd
had her children young too. Sometimes it
happened that way. Katha only hoped that
they hadn't suffered the same circumstances
that she herself had suffered. No! She
wouldn't think about those dreadful days, it
was better that way.

When the nurse spotted Edward she brought
Cecilia to Edward's side and Edward helped
the obvious invalid sit next to him. Carol
touched her grandmother's hand and Cecilia
smiled at her but then reached for Edward as
if she seen Carol. Carol sat down beside
Katha with Terrence on the other side of
Carol.

"Neddy I'm so glad you're here. This place
is scary and there are so many people,"
Cecilia said looking petrified.

Edward patted her hand and said soft inaudible words and Cecilia seemed happier. Audrey looked at her with disgust and then sat next to Terrence.

"Can we get on with this?" Audrey demanded, peevishly.

The lawyer soon dispensed with pleasantries and explained the disposition of the assets. Carol felt scared and didn't quite know what to say. All this stuff her parents had owned was now hers but what she wouldn't give to see them just one more time. Nothing had been said about where she would leave either. She wanted to stay with Grandma Katha and Grandpa Terrence. They had better not make her live with her horrible Aunt Audrey or she'd run away. Carol realized her thoughts had pulled her away from the conversations going on as she heard Katha ask, "So the house and all its contents were left in trust for Carol? And Harold left Carol a million dollars?"

"Yes, Harold did and her parents left the house contents and all the sums in their bank accounts to Carol. Plus the contents of her mother's apartment were left to Carol Banks as well. That is correct," the lawyer explained.

"What? But she's a kid why would they leave everything to Carol?" Audrey asked.

"And Carol has she's been left to Katha and me?" Terrence demanded ignoring his daughter's outburst.

"Don't be ridiculous Dad. You and you're new wife are way too old to look after a fifteen year old girl. I'm sure that Francine and Gerald would leave her to me or some other responsible adult in the family," Audrey stated.

"Audrey this is really none of your business. Katha and I are prepared to look after Carol. She is my great-granddaughter, after all," Terrence exclaimed.

"My point exactly! She's your great-granddaughter!! You are both in your twilight years. No offence, Dad, but the two of you could die tomorrow and where would Carol be then?"

"Audrey, you are quite aware that Francine wanted Dad to take care of Carol. I don't think it's any of your affair!!" Edward interjected.

"Really and will be my business when we have to find a home for the two of them, dad and step-mommy dearest because they can't take of themselves?" Audrey enquired with a slightly snotty tone in her voice.

"You always were a nasty spoiled brat, Audrey. Mom and Dad coddled you too much and you never learned compassion for anyone. Can't you see you are not only upsetting dad and Katha, but Cecilia and Carol too?" Edward demanded.

"And just what are you doing big brother to find the people that murdered my niece, her husband and my brother- in law? After all you are the police chief aren't you? How could you have let this happen?" Audrey countered.

"Audrey!!"Terrence began before Edward interjected, "Audrey I am doing everything possible to find them. Francine was my niece too. I loved her. She was one of the nicest sweetest women in this family."

"Who is that shrill woman, Edward? I don't think I like her. She yells a lot," asked Cecilia, "And where is my husband, Harold? He said he'd be right back, but that was awhile ago. Wasn't it?"

"It's okay Cecilia. "Edward reassured patting her hand then he explained gently, "This is our little sister, Audrey."

"Audrey? But Audrey's all grown up and she moved away. That's Frannie over there isn't it?" Cecilia asked pointing at Carol.

"No honey, that's your granddaughter Carol."

"But if that's Carol, where's my Francine? Frannie said she'd help Harold at the party and they'd both come back and see me in my room. Where are they?"

"I'm sorry Cece. Harold and Frannie are gone. I'm so sorry, sweetie."

"Gone where? He said he said they'd both be right back. He promised!!" Cecilia insisted.

"He's dead Cece and Frannie too," Edward explained gently.

"Nooooooo!!Why are you lying to me Edward? I know I have my moments but…" Cecilia cried.

"Really Edward; you hadn't told her yet?" Audrey interjected.

"He told her. She forgot, again," Carol explained.

"They're dead they're dead," Cecilia screamed and then wailing in cries that echoed through the room. Carol wanted to go to her but she knew from experience that would make this all worse, so she waited for the nurse to attend her grandmother. The nurse however looked alarmed and then Edward and the nurse then took Cecilia out of the room.

Audrey looked puzzled and then looked angry. Frankly Carol thought her Great-Aunt Audrey could use some chill pills.

"What the hell is wrong with Cecilia, Daddy?" Audrey demanded angrily.

"Aunt Audrey if you had been around the last year or called you'd know!! Grandma has Alzheimer's," Carol answered disgusted.

"She has what?" Audrey asks puzzled,

"Alzheimer's. Let me dumb this down for you so even you can understand, her brain is literally falling apart. She has bouts of confusion, irritability, aggression, and mood swings. Sorry to tell you this Great-Aunt Audrey, but she's dying. Most people don't live more than fourteen years after diagnosis," Carol said sadly.

"She's so young. Why didn't anyone tell me?" Audrey asked.

"Audrey you've been out of the country working all over the world for the last three years. This is the first time I've heard from you in three years so how could we have told you?" Terrence asked quietly in a soft, but frustrated voice.

"How can this even be possible she's only in her fifties? This happens to old people… like daddy!" Audrey exclaimed.

"It happens to all ages Audrey," Terrence explained.

"I looked up research on it can be genetic .You should be tested Aunt Audrey," Carol stated.

"What are you saying I could be as mindless as Cecilia? You nasty little…," Audrey bellowed.

"Audrey that is just atrocious. How dare you talk about your sister that way .What if she heard you?" Terrence admonished.

"She's lost her mind she'd forget the next minute," Audrey stated.

"What a beeyotch," Carol exclaimed under her breath.

"What did you say?" Audrey demanded.

"Nothing much." Carol replied covering, "Just that I had a stitch, you know in my side."

"Oh, okay then. As I was saying you two are too old to look after Carol. I should get custody."

"Over my dead body!" Katha stated angrily.

"That could be arranged," Audrey said grinning menacingly at Katha.

"Get the hell away from my wife, Audrey.
Don't you dare threaten her!" Terrence
bellowed, "I raised you better than this."

"Daddy can't you see this woman is trash.
She probably married you for your money,"
Audrey sniped.

"Actually Audrey, (not that it's any of your
business) but we both signed pre-nuptials.
You see Katha is actually richer than I.
She's been married a few times and has
wealth from her previous husbands and we
wanted to leave our moneys to our families,"
Terrence stated.

"Exactly previous husbands. The woman's a
black widow and don't get me started on her
granddaughter, Lily. I mean look at how
many husbands have died on her!!"Audrey
replied.

"I think you owe Katha and her family an
apology."

"I don't think so," Audrey replied defiantly.

Terrence raised an eyebrow.

"Over my dead body, dad."

"Audrey you are being incredibly insensitive to everyone here and until you apologise to my wife we have nothing to talk about," Terrence stated.

"Daddeeee.Please!!"Audrey whined like a little kid, then seeing that Terrence meant it she tried another tact, "Okay then, I'm sorry. Are you happy now?"

"I guess that will have to do," Terrence replied sounding annoyed.

"Can we get back to the will?" The lawyer asked sounding exasperated.

"Yes, please go ahead I'm sorry for the interruptions from my family," Terrence answered.

"The custody of the minor child Carol has been left to Terrence and Katha Stewart." The lawyer continued.

"So I guess that settles that Aunt Audrey," Carol exclaimed happily.

"Not really my opinion still stands they are too old to look after you Carol, and your inheritance. I'm contesting this," Audrey insisted.

"So that's what this is all about? You want money I'll be happy to give you some. Leave Carol out of your manipulations," Terrence exclaimed.

"I'll be in touch with my lawyer. Until then I'll see you all in court!" Audrey shouted triumphantly then strutted out of the office.

"Can she do that?" Carol demanded from the lawyer.

"She can try; but I don't think she'll win. Though if she finds the right judge she may try to use Terrence and Katha's age against them and it might work," the lawyer replied.

"Don't worry about her, Carol. Let's just all go home," Katha said trying to reassure Carol.

"Fine but I'll never live with her. I mean it!!!"Carol exclaimed.

Edward came back in minus Cecilia and asked, "What did I miss?

Regan explained and Edward put his arm around Carol and said, "I promise you, it will never come to that. Nobody can live with Audrey."

"We won't let that happen," Regan insisted.

"Thank you, Uncle Edward and Aunt Regan," Carol exclaimed.

Then Carol hugged Edward back before leaving with Katha and Terrence.

~0~

Chapter 4 – How do you solve a problem like Audrey?

Carol, Katha and Rose are in the surgery waiting area waiting to find out the outcome of Lily's surgery.

"Mom was lying wasn't she? This isn't just corrective surgery. It's something more serious that's why this is taking so long." Rose stated, obviously worried, then continued, "Tell me the truth Grandma Katha. What are surgery are they really performing?"

"Don't blame your mother I told her to tell you half-truths because she didn't want to worry you." Katha stated.

"So what is the surgery?" demanded Rose.

"They are fixing a problem with her heart," Katha admitted.

"Her heart, they are fixing her heart?" Rose said paling realizing that what she overheard was true.

"Yes, dear it takes awhile to do that kind of surgery. So don't be alarmed at the time length."

"I heard that, Aunt Katha. Lily told me she was having minor corrective surgery," Amelia bleated as she appeared coffee in hand.

"So it wasn't my age she just didn't want us to worry?" Rose stated.

"It seems so Rose. She really kept this secret. I had no idea," Amelia admitted.

Amelia then passed around the coffee she had brought back them back from the Tim Horton's, in the hospital.

"Where's Uncle Terrence?" Amelia asked.

"His sugars were a little high so the doctor recommended medicine and bed rest," Katha explained.

"Why isn't she out yet?" Rose asked.

"It does take awhile Rose," Amelia answered.

"We aren't stupid, or frail, she should have told us the truth," Rose cried.

"Sometimes we keep information that we think we'll hurt from our loved ones to protect them," Katha explained.

"Well I don't like it."

"It will be okay Rose. They are fixing it. They can't fix my Mom and Dad," Carol stated.

"I'm sorry Carol. You're right at least my Mother is alive."

"Mrs. Stewart, Rose, Amelia?" Doctor Terrell exclaimed coming up to them.

"Yes, I'm Mrs. Stewart and this is her daughter Rose and her cousin Amelia." Katha introduced.

"I'm Doctor Terrell. I assisted Doctor Abrahams. Lily is doing very well.

Obviously because it was heart surgery we will monitor her very closely the next day, or so but if all goes well we will be moving her from the cardiac unit to a normal hospital room and she will be home within a week," Dr. Terrell explained.

"Oh thank goodness. Can we see her?" Katha asked. "You can see her for a few moments. Just be aware that she may not realize you are there. We've given her some powerful pain killers, that will make her very groggy," Doctor Terrell answered.

Katha Amelia and Rose go into Lily's room one at a time to look at Lily then creep out quietly relieved.

"I need a chocolate bar," Rose stated.

"Here why don't you and Carol go get one," Katha stated.

Katha then handed Rose a twenty dollar bill.

"Thanks Grandma." They both said as they ran off.

"That was inventive .You want to tell me something Aunt Katha?" Amelia surmised.

"Yes, Audrey is a huge problem and Terrence I have been talking about her," Katha stated.

"What can you do?" Amelia asked.

"As much as Terrence and I would love to have Carol the court is going to look at our ages and Audrey will win unless we do something drastic," Katha stated.

"What drastic action?" Amelia asked.

"That's where you come in dear," Katha replied.

"Me? I don't understand."

"We want to adopt you and then have you adopt Carol," Katha answered.

"How will that stop Audrey?"

"Simple you'll have the same standing as Audrey because you will be her adopted sister." Katha explained, "We will back date the adoption and it will work.

"I don't understand how you can do that."

"Terrence has some old contacts that will do this for him."

"I still don't understand how will that make me eligible to adopt Carol?" Amelia enquired.

"Simple, Francine was a loving mother who thought of everything to protect her daughter. Francine left three other requests of people she considered to be outstanding to raise her daughter. These were written requests if for any reason we were considered too old or unfit then she asked that you or Edward adopt her daughter," Katha continued.

"I don't understand she hardly knew me."

"She knew you well dear. She admired your grit and determination to overcome tragedy. She also saw how you included her daughter in things you did with Rose," Katha explained, "She envied the love she saw in our little family. When she heard I was married to Terrence she was overjoyed for me. She decided then to give her marriage another try and by the time we asked if Carol could come on our wedding trip she saw it as the perfect opportunity for her second honeymoon."

"She really trusted me that much with her daughter?" Amelia asked.

"Yes, she did. I wish would could keep Carol but it won't be possible," Katha stated.

Carol coming back overheard.

"You don't want me?" Carol cried.

"Sweetheart we do want you but your Great-Aunt Audrey can use our ages against us and take you." Katha explained.

"But you can't let her have me .Please I'll do anything, but she's so mean. And she just wants my Mom and Dad's money," Carol exclaimed.

"Honey, that's what we are working on to prevent." Katha explained.

"If they say no to Aunt Katha and Uncle Terrence, I'm going to adopt you." Amelia stated.

"But how can you?"

"Aunt Katha and Uncle Terrence adopted me; making you my great niece therefore I have the same standing as Audrey, only more so as it seems your mother has asked me to adopt you and take care of you should Uncle Terrence and Aunt Katha be discriminated against because of their age."

Katha nodded her head.

"You'd do that for me?"

"Of course I would we love you Carol as much as Rose." Amelia stated, "Of course I would we love you Carol as much as Rose," Amelia stated,

"But where will I live, in your tiny apartment?" Carol asked.

"Actually we've already talked to Lily about this and if Amelia agrees we are going to buy a house we can all live in together," Katha answered.

"But I like my house," Rose complained then realizing how selfish that sounds she backtracked, "But if we live together we can be as close as sisters."

"Do you think the court will let Amelia adopt me?" Carol enquired.

"I don't see why not your mother left a letter stating she wished that Amelia adopt you not Audrey and because we've adopted Amelia, she is your family," Katha answered.

"Rose is right she said you were a crafty woman and that everything would workout okay," Carol exclaimed.

"Family sticks together and you're a Kelly now. We might as well go home for the night. Lily will rest and we'll see her in the morning." Katha stated," Maybe I could make my world famous Johnny Cake?"

"Yum! I'd like that!" Carol replied.

~0~

Chapter 5 - Investigation

The Happy Valley Police Precinct

"Oh good you're back partner,"

Kendall said.

"Yes, I'm back. So how was your Christmas?" Emmett asked.

"Busy. Poverty tends to escalate robberies and since I was covering for some other cops who wanted Christmas off I had to answer a couple of burglary calls."

"I was hoping it wouldn't be so active. Where were the burglaries?"

"The Corner Variety was robbed by a man in a Donald Trump mask."

"Not Santa Claus or one of his elves?" kidded Emmett.

"Nope. We got that guy two blocks over. Get this he dropped his wallet with his identification, so all I had to do was collect him at his apartment when he arrived home."

"He didn't offer you any resistance?"

"No. he actually just faked having a gun. He put his hand in his pocket with a pressure washer gun."

"A pressure washer gun?"

"Yes you know the kind you hose down your car with. It attaches on the end of a hose," Kendall explained.

"Some people!"

"Yep, think they can pull off a robbery with anything pretending to be a gun; but at least he couldn't hurt anyone with that. Did you hear about the other robbery?"

"No, I haven't caught up on any of the news here while I was away."

"Some guys robbed the gas station store on Fifth Street and Pine and killed the guy."

"Oh no, did we catch them?"

"Not yet but we have some good descriptions. One woman about thirty with reddish brown hair, height about five seven, and two males one about forty, standing six feet tall, weighing three hundred pounds brown stringing long hair to the shoulders with graying temples and the other approximately thirteen or fourteen years old five feet three skinny weighing about one hundred pounds with red hair. All of them white."

"Did you say thirteen?"

"Yes, we're seeking a thirteen year old murderer," Kendall replied.

"Accomplice you mean?"

"No, the other two were the accomplices. The kid shot and killed the proprietor."

"Good lord, they're getting younger every day. Any leads? Was it gang related?"

"Yes, we have a few leads. We don't know yet if it is gang related. Here read these while I drive the car."

Kendall then handed some reports to Emmett.

"So I ended up eating Christmas dinner at *Delightful Eats*."

"You didn't!" Emmett exclaimed.

"I did. Worse Christmas dinner I ever had. I'm lucky I didn't get food poisoning or something...,"Kendall broke off her and looked upset.

"Are you okay?"

"I thought your girlfriend would have told you. My uncle was killed along with my cousin Francine and her husband Gerald Banks, New Year's Eve, and you didn't come to the funeral," Kendall exclaimed.

"Banks... as in Carol's parents?"

"Yes, the very same."

"Someone murdered them?"

"They ate lemon squares that someone dropped off to my uncle New Year's Eve."

"How do you die from eating lemon squares?"

"I'm surprised you didn't know this my uncle was allergic to ginger and so was my cousin Francine. Carol is too. Uncle Harold was very vocal about food allergies and the types of food they served at City Hall, since he was elected."

"But Gerald wasn't allergic to ginger?"

"No," Kendall answered.

"So how did he die?"

"Francine took some of the squares home and ate one in the car. She crashed the car and they both died. Francine died from ingesting the square and Gerald from injuries from the accident when she crashed the car."

"Oh no, Carol; that poor kid and you too of course. Kendall, I'm sorry for your loss."

"I don't understand why Lily didn't tell you. I wondered why you didn't call or send flowers."

"Lily and I broke up." Emmett admitted.

"What a stupid beeyotch, dropping a great guy like you. I never liked her. Well, okay, I liked her; but not anymore if she dumped you, partner," Kendall quipped.

"She had good reason to dump me. There's a lot more to the story, but frankly I don't want to talk about it.

"You think you're going to get away with... we broke up; she had good reason to dump me... and not tell me anything?" Kendall complained.

"I don't want to talk about it. Just tell me what we are working on," Emmett stated.

"We are investigating the death of Harold Crimshaw."

"The mayor is dead?" Emmett interrupted shocked

"Haven't you read any news or heard anything I said?"

"Wait a minute your Uncle Harold is Harold Crimshaw?"

Kendall rolled her eyes.

"I'm sorry; of course the mayor is your uncle. I should have put two and two together. I've got to get my head in the game."

"What have you been doing since you and Lily broke up?"

"I took some extra time owed to me and I've just been hiding out licking my wounds since Lily left me," Emmett answered.

"It's probably good then that we have a murder to solve. My uncle Harold Crimshaw was dead as a door nail on New Year's Day," Kendall stated.

"You sound all broken up about him," Emmett commented.

"No, I'm not broken up about him. He was an asshole. The way he treated my Aunt Cecilia was abdominal. And before you asked I submitted an alibi. Number 1, I'm a terrible cook and two I was in Hawaii the last three weeks. All I care about is finding the person who killed my cousin and her husband," Kendall responded.

"We can't investigate they won't let us as your family."

"When has that ever stopped us?"

"Ah hell, they're Carol's parents, I should call Lily," insisted Emmett and then said, "No, I can't we're not speaking.

"I keep forgetting they are related to Lily; because her great-grandmother's married my grandfather," Kendall said pulling over in a parking lot to look through her notes, then she blurted, "I heard a rumour going around here at the station that that didn't make a lot of sense going around .Someone is rumouring that you have a seventeen year old son who's living with you."

"How did anyone find out so soon? This town! You'd think it would be easy to solve murders considering how much everyone is in everyone else business," Emmett replied angrily.

"Hey don't shoot the messenger. So it's true?" Kendall asked looking surprised.

"Yes, it's true."

"But you would have been younger than him when he was conceived."

"I can do the math Kendall."

"So that's why you broke up with Lily…"

"I'm not talking about that I told you. As for my son, his mother and he are living with me until she finds a place for the two of them."

"Oh the old ploy...can I stay with you? I'll move out as soon as I find a place. I hope you're not falling for that Emmett?" Kendall stated sounding annoyed.

"You know Kendall if I was it would be none of your business, but since I believe Sherry-Anne; she and my son Caleb can stay with me as long as they like," Emmett snarled.

"Just trying to look out for my partner. I'll drop it okay?" Kendall replied.

"I'm sorry too."

"Listen I'll tell you the whole story soon but I can't talk about this right now not if I want to get through the day."

"I understand and I really want to nail the bastard that killed...killed my family...members," Kendall said choking back tears and then covering but saying, "Sorry I tear up when I'm angry."

"I'm sorry for your family's loss Kendall but we'll find the asshole who murdered your uncle, and your cousins. Fill me in on the manner of the deaths and any other evidence."

Emmett looked over the files quickly and then said, "Death by ginger I still can't believe it. It must be hard to avoid during the Christmas season."

"I'm sure it was but they were both careful...too careful to accidently ingest something they knew would kill them. The problem is that new Assistant Crown Attorney Barbara Franks and her boss. She wants us to close the case and call it death by accident, simply to save her own position and march up the ladder," Kendall exclaimed.

"Why isn't Lily here? Why hasn't she taken this case? Is she too afraid of facing me?" Emmett demanded.

"Wow, who's full of himself now? Wait a minute, haven't you heard? Rumour is she had to have heart surgery," Kendall answered.

"Rumour or actual fact?"

"Grandpa told me that she's gone under the knife," Kendall admitted.

Emmett turned white and for a minute Kendall thought she'd have to pick him up off the floor of the squad car.

Taking a huge breath, Emmett asked, "Have you heard anything? Will Lily be okay?"

"I heard she'll be right as rain and home in a couple of days." Kendall replied, "You weren't planning on grovelling and going to the hospital were you?"

"No, I guess not; she wouldn't want to see me anyway," Emmett answered.

"You should still send flowers or something," Kendall insisted.

"Okay," Emmett said dialling a florist.

He then directed them to send a dozen red roses with a card that said...,

I'm sorry.

Please get well soon

Love Emmett

"Yes, that will win her over," Kendall said sarcastically.

"I hope so."

"You're so dense. The kid's mom is a problem. I'm sure."

"I'm not talking about what happened with Lily and I so quit fishing."

"You'll break sooner or later Emmett."

"Back to the case. Barbara Franks is the Crown attorney? She's filling in for Lily? Huh! She's very narrowed in her views. We may have some fun getting convictions with her in charge."

"That's probably why she warned Chief Stewart to close this now. She won't hear one word of how we think it could be murder. She just keeps insisting that we are grasping for straws. That chief Stewart is biased ...like she isn't?" Kendall griped, "Unless we find some evidence soon, she's going to totally shut us down and it's all because her boss said so and Barbara won't speak up and say it's murder because it might rock the boat."

"What a bitch!"

"You said it Emmett!! Some women would consider that a compliment that you were saying she was strong; but I know you mean it as an insult," Kendall replied.

"You have some pretty outlandish views; but I like them," Emmett answered.

"Right answer. That's why you love me as your partner. I'm different."

"Let's find some proof partner and put Barbara Franks' views to shame. Can we access the scene still?"

"Chief Stewart won't let anyone from the family go to the house, yet; so the scene is secure."

"What about Harold's wife, your aunt?"

"Cecilia lives in an expensive care facility for people with Alzheimer's."

"Poor woman, how will they explain this to her?" asked Emmett.

"I don't know. My aunt's very fragile."

Emmett and Kendall left the parking lot and Kendall drove talking.

"Wait until you meet the sister-in -law of the mayor," Kendall stated, "Now that woman is a piece of work. What a total bitch; she is. She puts on all the right words, but she never sounds sincere. She looked good for these murders, but she it seems she has an alibi. She was on a private plane coming in from Hawaii. She didn't even get in until seven a.m. at Happy Valley airport."

"You talk about your aunt that way?" Emmett asked.

"We're estranged. I can't stand her. I don't think anyone in the family can. I refuse to acknowledge her as my aunt. She may be my aunt by blood; but she's been sucking up all the air out of the world since she was born and making all of us miserable."

"Doesn't it seem weird that you should be investigating a case that involves your uncle and cousins?" Emmett asked.

"It wasn't daddy that assigned this case. I guess some people still don't know that my father is the chief of police. You won't tell them will you? Daddy is counting on me," Kendall begged.

"I guess as long as it doesn't affect the investigation it is okay. But there has to be some other suspects? Are we even sure what the ginger was in?" Emmett wondered.

"The new coroner says it was in some kind of sweet. I told you, he thinks it was an orange square," Kendall explained.

"What happened to my friend Dr. Andrew Piper?" Emmett inquired, "He's only forty. He can't be retiring."

"He's retiring. All those bodies piling up started to get to him I guess. He says that he has to have a life outside of his job, besides were you aware he was from a wealthy family? The guy is loaded. It's not like he has to work."

"What's he going to do with the rest of his life? Be bored?" Emmett asked.

"His grandfather is Gregory Hanks; CEO of Hank's a huge conglomerate that provides groceries across the country. He's retiring too and apparently handing over the reign to Andrew," Kendall explained,

"He's going from coroner to Grocer King?" Emmett said incredulously and then laughed.

Kendall honked the horn at a driver who cut suddenly in front of her.

"We should arrest that sucker," Kendall exclaimed.

"If we did that for every bad driver there would be no one on the road. Let it go

Kendall we have other fish to fry. It's really funny that the coroner is now a grocery King."

"If you think that's funny you should hear what they are calling the coroner's office now."

"I'll bite what are they calling it?" Emmett replied.

"They are calling it Davy Jones' locker. Get it? The coroner's name is Dafydd Jones. And he said call him Davy!" Kendall says

"Dafydd Jones is the new coroner? Son of a bitch, that asshole," Emmett snarled.

"You know him?"

"We met in London, Ontario. I didn't like him," Emmett answered cryptically.

"That guy is so hot he reminds me of a younger Pierce Brosnan. Every woman in the department is swooning over him and his accent," Kendall continued, blabbering on oblivious to Emmett's comment then she realized what Emmett had said, "But if you don't like him then I hate him too."

"Do we really need to talk about this Kendall?" Emmett interjected.

"Sorry, but we will run into the guy. I am taking us to interview Harold's secretary, one Grace-Ellen Singer. She just got back from Aruba. I don't think she's aware Harold is dead. She wasn't supposed to be back to work until next week, so that should give us an advantage over her knowledge that she keep back if she knew he was dead. She may be able to help us with motive and suspects," Kendall stated.

"Do you think she knows something thing about the squares?" Emmett queried.

"It could be. She was there at the house, about the time the squares were known to be there; but there was a lot of people at the Mayor's... er Great-Uncle Horace's party."

"So that makes her a suspect too. Let's hope this gives us the lead we need."

"Grace-Ellen lives in apartment three-oh-one." Kendall stated parking the car.

Emmett and Kendall exited the car and bounded up the stairs to the apartment door of Grace-Ellen Singer. Emmett knocked loudly the kind of police knock that rattles the walls. Kendall took a stance with gun drawn when there was no answer.

"Why did you need to draw your gun? Are you sure she's even home? When did she get in?" Emmett questioned.

"This is suspicious. Can't you feel it? Her flight got in at seven a.m. She should be home. I called and said we would be coming to talk to her at ten a.m. and it's ten oh one. I don't understand this," Kendall insisted.

"I'm beginning to have a bad feeling about this, too. Where's the supervisor's apartment?" Emmett stated.

"It's two-oh- one." Kendall replied.

"I'll stay here. You go get the super who will have a key to open this apartment," Emmett stated.

"Back in a jiffy."

A few moments later Kendall returned, a small wizened, older woman with a bunch of keys on a ring followed her. Her hair was white and hung in a long braid down her back and her teeth were yellow with nicotine stains as were her long arthritis riddled finger tips.

"Hi. I'm Trish Ellis," the five foot tall older woman with the curved back introduced herself.

"We are Sergeant Detectives Emmett Rogers and Kendall Evans," Emmett replied.

"Are you sure you had an appointment with Ms. Singer this morning? Maybe I should be waiting for a warrant?" Trish exclaimed.

"Ms. Ellis we could wait for one; but what if Ms. Singer needs help?" Emmett enquired softly using his abundant charm.

"I guess we could check and make sure she's okay. That is if I can stay with you and see you out. I wouldn't want to lose my job because I did this." Trish stated.

"I'd prefer you wait in the hall. If there's any danger or Ms. Singer needs help I'd want you to be safe," Emmett insisted.

"I guess that makes sense but you don't think she's in any real danger do you? She's such a nice lady."

"We just have to check ma'am," Kendall answered, "Please wait over there until we check this out."

"Police department, Ms. Singer?" Emmett exclaimed as Emmett, and Kendall entered the apartment to find things tossed all over the place.

The coffee table, an older heavy wooden one from the seventies has been upended like it's been thrown in rage. The sofa cushions are shredded, its foam in small pieces much like confetti spread across the floor. A coffee cup is turned upside down its contents embedded in the carpet.

A noise is heard behind them. Kendall turning around her gun still drawn she pointed it; only to find it was Trish that she pointed at.

Emmett too had his gun drawn and he placed it in his holster and insisted.

"I think you better leave now Ms. Singer. This is a crime scene now."

"But I can tell you..."

"Please, Ms. Singer, leave! We don't know if the person who did this is still here and we still have to find Ms. Singer."

Kendall escorted Trish to the front door and shut it. As they search the apartment they open the bathroom to find torn towels and cosmetics crushed into the floor. Each room they search is full of destruction, but where is Grace-Ellen Singer? They start searching under the furniture that has been moved.

Kendall took one bedroom and Emmett the other. Appliances were missing including the television.

Kendall creaked opened the closet of the bedroom she chose and demanded, "Emmett. I think you better come here. I've found Grace-Ellen Singer."

"Where?" asked Emmett running to Kendall.

As Emmett's eyes focused he saw that what he thought was crumpled pile of clothes in the closet is a woman bent over double, something dribbled from her mouth and death and had crusted on her lips.

"Are you sure this Grace-Ellen Singer?" Emmett demanded.

"Yes, she looks just like the picture I have of her here." Kendall said pulling out a picture that she compared, "Of course she was a lot less dead then."

Kendall looked around at all the destruction. A break and enter gone wrong? Turned deadly? Kendall thought and then dismissed it. There appeared to be more than one aspect at play here.

"What do you think killed her? I think there was more than one person here."

"Damn, we'll need the new coroner to confirm this guess; but I would say our killer has struck again. Grace-Ellen has been poisoned and maybe some housebreakers then broke in?" Emmett stated.

"That's what I was thinking but we need a team to confirm it. We could have Ms. Ellis identify her."

"In a while; after we process the scene," Emmett insisted.

"You're right; we wouldn't want her to contaminate the crime scene.

~0~

.

Chapter 6 – I don't want to be a witness

Katha jerked with a start as the

doorbell rang. Katha opened the door to reveal a police woman dressed in her uniform.

"Carol Banks?" asked the police officer not even looking up.

"May I see your badge?"

Constable Patricia Peters looked up and showed her badge.

\\

"Why Patricia, I didn't recognize you while you were looking at your paperwork. How lovely to see you again, what can I do for you Constable Peters?" Katha enquired.

"Ms. Kelly I didn't expect to see you here. How are you Ms. Kelly?" Patricia replied.

"I'm very well. Please call me Katha, I guess you haven't heard I got married to Terrence Stewart," Katha answered.

"No, I hadn't… wait a minute is that the chief's father?"

"Yes, dear, Terrence is Edward's father. Since Carol's parents died; Terrence and I have been appointed temporarily Carol's guardian."

"I really have to deliver this to her personally," Patricia replied hesitantly.

"She's fifteen years old." Katha protested, "I suggest you tell me what all this is about. Please Patricia for old time's sake?"

"Well I guess I could leave the subpoena with you; but you have to sign for it and make me a guarantee that Carol will appear as a witness tomorrow."

"Carol was a witness to what? What is this all about?" Katha demanded.

"Remember the Scholar killer, Dr. Thomas and his wife?"

"You mean former Principal Janet Carol Thomas?"

"The two of them murdered Alexander Scholar," Patricia said bluntly.

"No, that's not what Amelia and Carol said. That poor Mr. Thomas was pulled into it with that murderous cheating wife of his," Katha stated.

"Well I guess that's why she's being called to testify tomorrow. Carol Banks and Amelia Kelly are receiving a subpoena today to testify tomorrow at the trial of Jane Carol Thomas," Patricia exclaimed, "You as a lawyer Ms. Stewart must realize and then caution Carol against speaking about this case with Amelia Kelly or anyone else before she testifies tomorrow."

"I'll make sure she doesn't; but it won't be easy. Amelia is my adopted daughter. She's moving in to our home. Amelia is hoping to get custody of Carol if all else fails with our suit. Luckily for us she doesn't move in until next week." Katha responded, "Can you stay for a drink? Would you like tea or coffee and some cookies?"

"Why not? I like a coffee. I could use a break."

"How is your battle going?"

"What battle?"

"Being taking serious at the police station?" Katha replied, handing Patricia coffee as they sit down and some cookie on a plate.

"You wouldn't believe what jerks some of those guys can be. First they tell me my uniform is too loose and to have it tailored and then when I do the guys stare and the women frown," Patricia said dropping cookie crumbs down her front.

Katha tried not to laugh. Patricia seemed like a big kid and yet she was a police woman. The older Katha got the younger the people her around were getting. Maybe that's what kept Katha young. Yet no matter how you looked at it women were being harassed in the work place. That wasn't acceptable maybe she should lay a suit against the Happy Valley Police force? She still had her ability to practice law but it would require a great deal of money and only a big firm could handle this. Maybe she should put Patricia in touch with her friend at Dunham, Dunham and Pride in Toronto?

"I understand dear. Some women don't help the same gender at all they just make it worse." Katha prodded, "Do you want me to put you in touch with a lawyer to address this with a suit against the police department?

"I can't make a big case about this .If I make waves then it will be worse for me. You must have come across that in your career so you know what I'm speaking about. Actually I'm thinking about leaving the police department and finishing my law degree," Patricia stated.

"Do you want to be lawyer or is it just the job getting to you?" Katha enquired.

"No, I want to help people as a lawyer. I would like to work in the crown attorney's office," Patricia explained.

"You could do a lot of good there. My granddaughter Lily is the crown attorney there," Katha stated, "I'll make some calls. Maybe when you're finished you can article there."

"Thank-you I appreciate that. I really have to go. I've done my duty and served the subpoena on you for Carol see that she arrives a half an hour before court starts at 9 a.m.," Patricia cautioned getting up to go.

"You give me a call back in a few days and I'll see what I can do about the articling job."

"I have to go serve this subpoena to Amelia Kelly. She lives in the apartment over the garage two doors down?" Patricia continued.

"That's correct and don't worry I will make sure Carol's at court," Katha exclaimed.

"Thanks Katha, for everything."

Patricia then walked down the sidewalk to Amelia's home.

"Carol?" Katha yelled.

"What Grandma Katha?" Carol asked.

"A policewoman I knew was here. She gave me this subpoena to have you testify tomorrow at the Thomas trial," Katha stated.

"Oh do I have to? That was awful .That awful woman wanted to kill me and her husband was that much better. I mean I felt sorry for the guy but he wanted to kill me too," Carol whined.

"I know they did pumpkin and that's why you have to be very brave and testify to what they did and said," Katha explained.

"I'm going to call Aunt Amelia," Carol insisted.

"I'm sorry honey, but you can't talk to her until after you testify," Katha stated.

"That's not fair why are you keeping me from Aunt Amelia?" Carol responded angrily.

"It's the rules honey. You aren't allowed to talk to other witnesses until after the testimony is given," Katha explained.

"I still don't think it's fair. I can still talk to Rose can't I?" Carol asks

"Yes, dear, you can talk to Rose; but maybe not about your testimony." Katha answered, "I will be there with you through the whole thing tomorrow, I promise."

"Yah, whatever. I'm going to see Rose I promise if see Aunt Amelia I won't talk to her. I hope she won't think I'm mad at her," Carol responded by grabbing her coat and going through the front door.

I hope that Carol's okay .She seems so mad at the world. Who can blame her all those people around her dying and now this reminder of her kidnapping. Not to mention that awful Audrey trying to take her from us .I wish she'd see that nice Dr. Georgia Jeffries who took over from Doctor Ellen Jones. She is hurting straight to the core; but she won't let us in. Maybe she'll confide in Rose .I hope so before Carol bursts from keeping in all that hurt and anger.

Oh well sooner or later she'll realize we are there for her. Katha thought to herself. In the meantime we will be there for her love her and support her sooner or later she'll come around.

~0~

Chapter 7 - Impact

Carol and Amelia had gotten through their testimony and surprisingly the trial had stopped when Doctor Thomas had turned to Mrs. Thomas and whispered in her ear. They then stood up and both said they wanted to change their plea to guilty. That changed everything the judge said sentencing would be in three weeks and that they would be held in jail until then.

Carol decided to skip school. Who cared about it anyway?

Amelia beckoned her offering Carol a ride and then Amelia drove her there so she went in and pretended she cared about the history lesson Ms. Bates was giving.

School was a drag how was she supposed to concentrate when they were not any sooner finding her grandfather, mom and dad's murderer then they were a few weeks ago. Hard to believe it had been almost five weeks since they'd been murdered.

Oddly enough though Carol had won many contests over the last few weeks; some she'd forgotten that she'd had even entered. They were only things and she couldn't even muster up any happiness at winning maybe Rose was correct and she should go to bereavement meetings but she felt like she could never talk about any of her feelings with anyone. Why was she so angry at Rose? Rose was her best friend and had offered her many opportunities to vent and how had Carol rewarded her? With yelling sniping and a lot of other meanness. Rose had Lily. Granted Lily wasn't her biological mom; but she was every inch her mother. Carol had no one.

Okay, so Grandma Katha and Grandpa Terrence were trying to adopt her or get someone to adopt her. But really it was like she was a puppy no one wanted except Aunt Audrey who wanted her only for the money her parents and Grandpa Crimshaw had left her.

"Carol Banks have you been listening at all? I asked you a question young lady," Ms. Bates interrupted.

"Sorry Ms. Bates. I have a headache, Carol lied, but then it came true and Carol found she did have one.

"You can be excused Carol," Ms. Bates answered.

Carol collected her things as Rose looked over her eyebrow raise. Take that Rose Brooksfield you don't know everything, Carol thought.

Carol needed time to think, be alone and cope without Rose sticking her nose in maybe she go to Grandpa's and see if she could sniff out some clues. She taken the key from Great-Uncle Edward's desk drawer in the study when she'd visited there. Carol had made a copy and then returned the key the same day. Great-Uncle Edward would never even know Carol copied it.

Carol took the bus over to grandpa's house and wandered up the driveway watching carefully to make sure no one saw here. Breaking the police tape she entered the house. Carol thought that other than the dust that had gathered the house looked exactly the same like grandpa would come out of his office and any minute.

Carol didn't know quite what she was looking for but she know what it was if she saw it. She'd solve these murders and make the person or persons who killed her parents and grandfather pay. She looked in the kitchen and saw foods still sitting on the kitchen table. Gross hadn't anyone cleaned up?

Then she realized of course they hadn't
cleaned up they had tested the foods of
course and determined that they had been
poisoned. If Caleb hadn't told her what his
dad had said she wouldn't have known that
it was the lemon squares that ad killed them
but where was he container? Caleb said the
cops hadn't found it and it didn't appear to
be here. Had the dish been washed and put
in the cupboard?

Carol opened the cupboards but there were
no containers in the cupboard they all
appeared to be dirt and filled with food on
the table.

EW, the food would soon attract bugs didn't
they know that? Why hadn't anyone cleaned
up? Carol dumped the containers of food
into the garbage and then washed each dish
and dried them putting them back into the
cupboard. Carol then wipe the table and
swept the floor. Grandpa would be happy
the place looked normal again. Then Carol
started crying grandpa, mom and dad would
never see this place again.

Carol grew angry and started throwing the plastic containers out of the plastics drawer. A few minutes later she laughed her rampage didn't make her feel any better. Carol picked up the containers none of them were broken or dirty. She laughed as she put them back in the drawer. Grandpa would have been horrified but mother would have laughed.

She had to find that container that held the lemon squares where could it be? Her headache was raging now no wonder she couldn't think she'd go home to Katha's have a nap and think on it.

~0~

Emmett and Kendall

Emmett and Kendall were tired after handling the paperwork for the Singer murder but they wanted to solve these murders. Obviously it was connected to the Crimshaw/Banks murders but how? And who had committed these murders was it more than one person or were they trying to throw the investigators off the scent by making it seem they were more than one perpetrator.

Kendall delved into the information they had and logged all the information into the computer .She then sent the same file to Emmett.

Each of them sat at their desks reading over the files.

"Anything new on the Singer murder and how it connects to the murder of the mayor and his family, Emmett?" the police chief asked.

"We're working on it, chief," Kendall answered before Emmett could; "We're hoping to have a few more leads after we review our notes.

"Good keep on it this is an important case I'm trusting you two with but if you don't get leads soon I'll have to transfer the case to someone else," Chief Edward Stewart exclaimed loudly.

"Understood Chief. We'll solve this case soon," Emmett replied.

"One week that's all you've got," Edward said as he walked away.

"Rough," Roy Callahan exclaimed.

"Keep waiting Roy will bag the solve," Kendall responded.

"I'm sure you will but I'll keep my notepad ready."

"Do that but it will stay empty," Kendall stated walking away then turning back to Emmett she said, "Come on partner I have an idea."

~0~

Chapter 8 - A Killer's View

That was too close. I barely got out of that apartment complex before they arrived. I had to keep alert no one could find out what I had done. Harold was an ass of the first order. He had deserved to die and now he had forced me to take not one, but four lives. Of course Grace-Ellen Singer wasn't a nice person so that had made it easier. She had been blackmailing Harold for years…years. Her vacation that she taken, had been a reward for that blackmail. Grace-Ellen Singer knew what the cretin was about but instead of taking her evidence to the police she'd chosen to profit from his crimes. Grace- Ellen was a Judas to all women. And really didn't Judas deserve to die?

Grace-Ellen, what a foolish woman!! She had welcomed me into her apartment offered me tea like she knew me. She didn't know me. As soon as she had turned her back I slipped the poison into the tea. She must have ruined her taste buds; because she didn't even make a murmur about the taste. She just kicked it back and asked for more. It was so damn easy. And yet there was a little lingering guilt; I had to keep reassuring myself that she deserved what she got. Dispensing with the evidence washing the tea things leaving no trace of myself had been hard. The gloves I had brought had helped though and the wipes to wipe all the things I had touched down. I had vacuumed the floor and the sofa making sure I had left not trace behind. Then I disposed of the vacuum bag.

Really who used vacuum bags anymore? I guess I was just lucky Grace-Ellen had. I had taken that with me and disposed of it in the dumpster next door. The garbage people were already there. They wouldn't find it. So who had tossed the joint? Crap I forgot to lock the door it had to have been dug addicts searching for cash or goods.

Why had I become prey to such a person? He was truly evil and despite this act of mine killing him I was a good person. It was too bad that I had been forced to kill Harold's son-in-law and daughter by accident, but really greed had gotten them killed not me. If Francine had eaten what wasn't hers, they wouldn't have died. From all I had heard Gerald was a carbon copy of his father-in- law. So Gerald deserved his fate I guess it was true woman married their fathers. Francine had. Francine death nagged at me though... poor dumb woman. Loyal to the end she took the cheater back!! So maybe I did her a favour?

I felt extremely guilty about Carol, though Francine's daughter. She seemed like a nice kid and now she had no parents and that was my fault. Poor Carol! Just a few months ago she had been kidnapped by a murderer. What a rotten life and I had contributed to make that worse. Maybe if she got an unexpected gift something to cheer her but what?

She hung out a lot with that girl Rose Brooksfield. Nice kid that one, despite her background. Rose's birth parents were terribly evil, immoral people. Really serial killer or no serial killer, Brad Owens had done the kid a favour getting rid of those around them that would harm them. Rose was a good influence on that Carol. It must because Lily Wentworth Brooksfield had raised her in her formative years. Carol could have turned out like that cousin of hers Daria Brown. Now that girl was a piece of work. Was that because she lost her mother? Or was it her cop father flitting around from woman to woman?

Could that happen to Carol? Could she turn into a Daria? What if I caused Carol to go off the rails and be like her cousin, Daria? Then she'd be like me changed and slightly broken. This wouldn't do. I had to do something for her.

A concert?

Would she like a concert ticket to see a popular group? Who did the kids like today anyway? I'd Google one of the top acts on the music chart. Hmm Lady Gaga I'd heard of her. It was not my type of music but the kids seemed to like her. Was she coming to Happy Valley? Figures she wasn't; but she was coming back to Ontario in March this year. No, that wouldn't work! But I'd find some act Carol would like. I didn't want these tickets traced back to me either. So I had to figure out how to buy them without anyone tracing it back to me. It wasn't possible without exposing me as the donor. So maybe a local group the kids liked. This would take some work and some time. In the meantime make sure there was no evidence that could trace back to me in any of the killings was my top priority.

Crap! Shit!!! Fuck!!!!That damn dish I brought the squares in was missing. I had to find it. It could nail me; reveal me to the world as the murderer I am. Calm down I told myself. I wouldn't be found out. I was too smart for them.

They thought they were so smart; but I was a member of the smartest people in the world. My IQ was higher than Einstein. It was good to hide all those smarts under a bushel. People underestimated me and that gave me the edge over them. I would triumph over them as I had triumphed over the evil that was Harold. All was well I could still breathe fresh air untainted by prisoners and I would continue to do so. I would solve the dish problem and all would be well. After all those people deserved what they got even the bible spoke about greed. I was an avenging angel.

~0~

Chapter 9 - Deception

Carol was sick of school and the whispers; wondered how did Rose ever put up with it? She'd left early yesterday because of her headache; but that didn't help her they'd found something else to whisper about claiming Carol had a nervous breakdown. She wished the world would go away. Why did she have to go to school anyway? Didn't anyone care that her parents were dead? And she was just supposed to put it out of her head and concentrate on school? Who gave a damn about history or equations there was a mad man out there who had killed her parents and her grandfather,

This place was called Happy Valley they should have called it Murder Valley. People kept dying in town like flies and now her parents? Why hadn't they caught the culprit? It was probably because that stupid Emmett Rogers was too obsessed with Caleb's mother that man-stealing bitch .He'd better start working harder and find this dreadful person. Rose was annoying her too. She was all I'm so sorry Carol but all she did was go on and on about how her father had died too. Rose had two mothers and she had none! None!!

Who could have murdered such wonderful people like her Mom and Dad? Grandpa had lots of enemies maybe her parents were killed by accident? No one would talk to her about the murder and she needed to know some of the details. Grandma Katha was bugging her sending her to a shrink like that would make everything better.

Nothing would ever be better again. And as long as that killer was out there Carol was scared. What if the killer came after someone she loved again? She had wondered if it was somehow payback from Janet Thomas for convincing Dr. Thomas to turn on her; but unless she had hired a hit person. She was terrified and no one even noticed didn't anyone even care about her now her parents were gone?

And where was her best friend Rose… her I'll always be beside you, anyway? Carol looked around and spotted her with of all people Caleb Rogers. Why were their heads together? They were together yesterday too. What had happened? His stupid father had cheated on Rose's mother. Had she no loyalty? Caleb had his arm around Rose. Carol eyes narrowed Rose had not said a word to her about Caleb and yet her she was acting like they were together. Together, together!!Like Caleb was her boyfriend. Some best friend, if Rose was keeping a secret like that. She walked out of the cafeteria.

"I think it will work." Caleb commented, "Look Carol believed we are together."

"She stalked off; she's mad. Really you think we can get them back together? Why can't I tell Carol?" Rose asked.

"I hate keeping anything from Carol; but if she believes it every else will too," Caleb added, "I should be cheering on my mom. Isn't it the dream of every kid to have their parents together?"

"Yes, it is. So why are you doing this then?"

"Because my dad is miserable and my mom is putting on a great act; but I don't think she really loves my dad. Dad is miserable. I know Mom would like to get back with him, but she's had two months and he's not falling for anything she does. I'm starting believe she did something because it was totally out of character of the guy I've gotten to know as my Dad. He wouldn't be such a horn dog and sleep with my mom while being practically engaged to your Dad," Caleb answered.

"You think she did something? What could she have done?" Rose asked surprised.

"I don't want to talk about it. Forget I mentioned anything," Caleb covered quickly.

"No, you opened that up. Tell me what you think Caleb," Rose begged.

"If I tell you will you promise not to do anything to my mom no matter what?" Caleb begged.

"It's that bad? Well okay as long as she hasn't committed murder I guess I wouldn't harm your mom. That's what you meant isn't it like turn her in for a crime, or something? You think she committed a crime?" Rose enquired then looking at Caleb she continued, "You do? Did she drug your Dad is that what you suspect?"

"She's nurse she has access to drugs and Dad would do this. He said he was drinking and woke up with her. You put something in a drink and ....."Caleb breaks off here

"The date rape drug Roofies? You think Sherry-Anne roofied Emmett?"

"Yes," Caleb replied quietly.

"That's pretty serious .Caleb that's a crime how could she have done that to your Dad?" Rose asked.

"I don't know; but Mom wasn't quite herself after hearing about Aunt Betty and her Dad," Caleb excused.

"Yes I guess but to do that... to someone she says she loves…"

"I know it's awful. That's why I don't want to believe she did this. Dad is so unhappy. I heard him talking to his partner Kendall Evans .He snuck up and was outside your Mom's hospital room and made sure she was okay. He saw her with that Dr. Jones guy and left after talking to her doctor," Caleb replied.

"That guy is such a dork." Rose stated dismissing Dr. Jones, "He has a movie star face but he's got nothing going on upstairs."

"I take it you don't like him then?" Caleb says hiding a laugh

"I hate him. He always like "Aren't you a nice little girl. Your mom is so lucky to have a nice little girl like you," Rose stated angrily.

"Mom is so busy trying to pin Dad down she hardly ever speaks to me," Caleb complained.

"Your Dad should be with my mom and if they had to talk to each other because their kids were involved...?"Rose implied.

"It will mean a lot of pretending. Are you okay with that given the way we feel about each other?" Caleb asked.

"Even though it will be like kissing my big brother," Rose stated.

"I know you felt like my little sister when we kissed that one time. It just didn't seem right. So are you going to be able to act your way through this?"

"I thought about being an actress once .Want to see how convincing I am?" Rose asked kissing Caleb full on the lips passionately.

"That will do it," Caleb says "Look at Carol she looks puzzled it is working."

"So she's back? Good because good actress or not this is hard. Now shall we walk to class hand in hand?" Rose enquired grinning widely

"That should work."

Carol stared at Caleb and Rose. They were kissing and now they were walking hand in hand were they a couple? Rose hadn't told her anything. She felt betrayed and oh so alone. No one gave a damn about her Rose was moving on with her life she had a boyfriend and not just any boyfriend someone that both knew and cared about as a friend.

At this moment she hated Rose. She hated Caleb .She hated the whole damn world. If only there was something that would take all this pain away. Something that would make her forget that no one loved her no one cared that her parents were gone. Drugs booze? No she'd find something else. Something fun; without that two-faced Rose.

"Hey Carol want to come to a party tonight?" Bobby Brantford asked.

"Where and what time?" Carol enquired, stunned that Bobby the guy she had been interested in so long was asking her to a party.

"It's at Nathan Patel's," Bobby admitted.

"Oh I don't know if I want to go there." Carol replied.

"Are you chicken or just a nerd or both? So he'll have a little beer," Bobby taunted.

"I'm not chicken .I'm just not fond of Nathan .He's a pervert," Carol answered.

"I heard you punched him a few months ago," Bobby stated.

"Yes, I did. He's a pervert. I don't think he'd want me at his party."

"He said I could bring a date and you're my date. Please Carol?" Bobby begged.

"I guess if you put it that way, and you keep him away from me. What time?" Carol enquired, smiling

"I'll pick you up at eight p.m. Where are you staying?" "With my great grandmother it's nine hundred sixty- eight Applewood Road but I'll have to sneak out .I'll meet you at the Dot Cafe okay?" Carol replied.

"Okay sounds good see you at eight. I've got to get to class."

Things were looking up, Carol thought. Bobby Bradford had asked her out. She wanted to tell Rose; but Rose had her own secrets so why shouldn't Carol have hers. Carol smiled two could play the secrets game. That would fix that rotten Rose for not sharing.

She would be going to a party with Bobby Bradford the quarterback. She was so excited. She'd tell Rose afterwards and make Rose sorry that she didn't share with Carol. Rose would be so jealous that she didn't get an invitation. Carol was with one of the most popular guys in school take that Rose.

~0~

Sometime later in the day

"Hello Rose .So what precipitated your visit here today?" Dr. Jeffries asked.

"I don't know." Rose replied hesitating.

"You do know you had something you needed to talk about so you came here."

"I'm tired." Rose admitted

"Tired of what?"

"I'm tired of pretending that everything is fine that I'm okay," Rose answered.

"And you are not fine?"

"No I'm not my Dad died and I feel so empty so lost. I pick up the phone to call him to tell him something at his office. Or I go to the mall and I see him but it's not him. And I'm so damn mad at him. Why was he cheating on my mom with Amber? My mom deserved so much better .She married him and took me as her daughter. Why did he do that? He said he loved us," Rose cried angrily.

"People make mistakes Rose it is a part of life."

"That wasn't just a mistake, he betrayed us. And then Mom starts dating the cop that helped find the guy that killed my Dad and he cheats too. How can you trust any guy? I'm thinking and," Rose hesitated, and then deciding to continue she said, "You have to keep what I say confidential right?"

"Yes, as long as it doesn't endanger you or someone else," Dr. Jeffries stated.

"Caleb Rogers says Emmett didn't purposely cheat on my mom he says he thinks his mom drugged him," Rose confessed.

"Does he have any proof of this?"

"No, but he thinks his mom would do this. She needs a shrink. Her thinking is all confused and she's been through stuff she can handle," Rose stated.

"Does he believe she will do this again?"

"I don't think so."

"How can he be sure if she's not thinking clearly?"

"He is. My point is people are cruel you know. And my Mom has been through so much. She should be happy and this woman has stolen her happiness. I should want her to be with Emmett …"

"But you're not happy about this because you're not ready for her to move on and marry anyone else."

"How did you know that?"

"Rose we've talked about this. It is not your job to make everyone happy. You have the right to your own happiness and you don't have to worry that people not being happy will make them leave you," Dr. Jeffries stated.

"Are you sure?" Rose asked in a small voice.

"Yes. Your hour is up but if you feel like this again. I want you to call my secretary and make an appointment. I want you to tell yourself this mantra. I can be sad if I need to be. I am not responsible for anyone's happiness but my own!" Dr. Jeffries stated, "Now I want you to keep taking your medicines okay? And if you feel you need to see me come back immediately. Understand?"

"I'll take them, even though they sometimes make me feel sluggy," Rose agreed.

"Goodbye Rose I'll see you next week, the same time." "Thanks. See you next week." Rose replied, looking at her watch and seeing it was eight-thirty p.m...

She called home but received no answer. She called Grandma Katha's and gets no one answered. She called Carol's cell and it goes to voicemail.

"Where is everybody why weren't they answering their phones?" Rose wondered, and then she dialled Caleb, "Hello Caleb. No one is answering at home do you think you could come pick me up with your mom or dad's car at my doctor's office? It's at 156 Acorn Street."

"Sure no problem, I'll come get you Rose and take you home until someone arrives at your house. If that is okay?"

"Thanks Caleb you're a peach." Rose retorted happily.

A short time later they arrived at Emmett's house and entered the house.

"My parents aren't home. Mom's working she got a job as a nurse at Happy Valley hospital and Dad's trying to find the killer that killed Carol's family members." Caleb explained, "But I'm sure it's okay because you're like my sister."

"I don't know where everyone could be," Rose stated

"Does your Grandma Katha have some committee meeting or something?" Caleb enquired.

"Oh, I forgot she and Grandpa Terrence are involved with the hospital board. They had a meeting scheduled tonight. How could I have forgotten?"

"And your Aunt Amelia?"

"Aunt Amelia is at her store."

"So you do know where everyone is."

"Where could Carol be though?"

"I can't believe I forgot Carol. Oh dear you don't suppose she went to that party do you?"

"What party? I didn't hear about any party."

"Nathan Patel was throwing a party tonight. I hate that guy he's such a worm," Caleb answered.

"Why would she go to that party? She hates him. She threw a drink at him for me," Rose stated.

"Why did she throw a drink at him?"

"Let's just say he deserved it and leave it at that."

"Such of a bitch. I should knock that asshole's block off. I heard rumours but…"

"He didn't drug me but he did touch me indecently."

"I knew there was a reason I hated him. I'd like to hit that smug veneer off his face."

"Carol handled it and it is over."

"I'm kind of worried about Carol. She's been a bit off since her parents were killed."

"I should have been paying attention to her .I should have gave her more time. She probably was desperate for company and went to this party after she saw us faking being together. This is all my fault," Rose stated.

"Nathan's parents are out of town .That party could get wild," Caleb says worried

"What can we do?"

"We could go get her," Caleb answered, "If she's there."

"Where else could she be?"

"Let's just go to Nathan's." Caleb stated, "If she's not there then no harm, no foul. But we need to check it out. Nathan is dangerous."

"Okay then let's go. Now!" Rose insisted.

~0~

Chapter 10 - Busted

Sometime later

"Rogers here," Emmett answered while driving his patrol car.

"There's a 142 at 1205 Apple Street."

"Jenni, why are you calling me about an unlawful assembly? Can someone else handle it? Is there a cop down?" Emmett asks

"No, but your son was there and…,"Jenni answered tepidly

"Caleb was at an unlawful assembly? What kind of disturbance?" Emmett asked worried.

"There was a keg party at that residence and the kid must have invited everyone at Facebook because five hundred people showed up. The place was trashed there were fights going on and underage drinking. Our officers seized ecstasy, pot, LSD, and cocaine to list a few of them," Jenni answered.

"Caleb was there? That doesn't sound like him."

"The officer who was sent to the scene Patrolman Alan Barnes asked me to let you know. He also wanted me to let Ms. Rose Brookfield and Ms. Carol Banks was found there as well," Jenni stated, "I've been unable to reach their guardians."

"Good grief; are you telling me the girls were there too?"

"Patrolman Barnes brought them in they haven't been charged or logged in but he put them in a holding cell to scare them."

"Thanks Jenni and tell Alan thanks for not laying charges. I'll help take custody of the situation and put the fear of god in them. I'm in my way in."

"You heard Kendall?"

"Teens! I remember my first kegger."

"Keggers? They probably don't even call it that anymore. I wonder why Caleb didn't let me know about this party?"

"Did you tell your dad your whereabouts when you were teen?" Kendall laughed.

"Actually I did. I never let my parents worry," Emmett replied.

"Oh, you were Dudley Do-right even as a kid," Kendall smirked.

"So?"

"So most kids aren't like you. You've seen them when we've patrolled. It's a game to see how much you can hide from your parents," Kendall explained.

"What have I got myself into?" Emmett asked.

"Parenting it's never easy, but you're a good guy you'll manage partner," Kendall reassured, "Good thing our shift is done so you can scare the brats straight."

Emmett arrived at the Happy Valley police station followed by Kendall. Kendall veered off into the locker room; but Emmett continued walking and was surprised to hear Jenni being yelled at the front desk, "Carol's my great niece. I'm her great-aunt of course you can release her to me."

"You are not her guardian," Jenni stated.

"I'm the crown attorney Barbara Franks. What is going on here?" Barbara interceded, coming up behind Emmett.

"Please let me handle this," Emmett insisted.

"You better Detective Rogers. We can't have someone causing such a ruckus in the police station, even if she is the police chief's sister," Barbara says going into the cells to see a suspect.

"I told you, I'll handle this. There won't be any trouble will there Ms. Stewart?" Emmett stated, smiling at Audrey.

"Hello Emmett. I haven't seen you in years you. I would hardly have recognized you. You wouldn't believe what I've been going through," Audrey prattered.

"Maybe I can help with this. I know Carol."

"You will? Thank-you. Why the court thought an old woman could look after a wayward teen, I'll never know!"

"I hear you have applied for custody. It's a huge responsibility. I ought to know I just found out I have a teen son."

"Wow, we really have to catch up. How's your sister Teresa?"

"She's fine. She lives in Sudbury with her husband Jason and son, Greg," Emmett replied.

"I always thought you were acute little kid; but you've grown up into a really handsome man!" Audrey gushed, "So you're a top cop?"

"I'm a detective .You do realize I can't give you Carol don't you?" Emmett cutting to the chase.

"Why the hell not?" Audrey asks "Those two old farts are looking after her and look what happens she's unsupervised and goes to a wild party. I want my great-niece and I want her now!"

"Audrey, you don't have legal custody I have to give her to Katha and your Dad, Terrence," Emmett stated, quietly.

"Fine, but I want this on record. I'm going to use this to get custody of my niece," Audrey insisted.

"Audrey really!! How is this best for Carol? She hardly knows you," Emmett demanded.

"Carol can't remain with those two old people. She's young and they can't possibly understand her," Audrey answered.

"Please think about what is best for Carol."

"I am and it isn't two old farts stuck in the last century." "Katha and Terrence are wonderful people; if you get to know them," Emmett insisted.

"Then Daddy has changed since he married Katha; because he was great with giving me money and patting me on the head, but he was never there for me emotionally. I won't have that for Carol. She derives better."

"Katha would never let that happen."

"It seems you know this stepmom Katha better than me then. She seems cold and grasping to me." Audrey concluded, "Tell my Dad when you see him that would you? I trust you to handle this Emmett. You were always a good kid despite your family situation."

"Good-bye Audrey."

Emmett went into the holding cells to find Caleb in one cell and Rose and Carol in the other.

"Dad I'm sorry really I can explain," Caleb began before he was interrupted by Carol.

"It's my fault Mr. Rogers. I'm sorry I just wanted to forget about everything and when Bobby asked me...He asked me to go to this party. Well I said yes, but he was such a creep no wonder he hangs out with Nathan. If Caleb hadn't rescued me....," Carol rambled and then began crying.

"It's okay Carol we got there in time," Rose insisted.

"Are you telling me this boy tried to rape you Carol?" Emmett asked alarmed.

"I don't know. I said no, but he pulled me into a bedroom and he hesitated and wouldn't let me out right away when I said no again. So I guess no. But I was so scared," Carol replied.

"What about that other guy I pulled off you near the front door," Caleb says pointedly.

"He ripped my shirt. If you hadn't stopped him...,"Carol cried breaking off.

"Do you know who this guy was Carol? Would you like to lay charges?" Emmett inquired his voice sounding low and strangely quiet.

"No, I just want to forget this night ever happened," Carol answered.

"Can we go home or are we being charged Emmett?" Rose enquired.

"You've all be released into my custody," Emmett stated, "We'll talk all about this later Caleb and I'm sure Katha Terrence and Lily will have lots to talk to you to about again."

"Do we have to tell them?" Carol asked.

"Your Aunt Audrey already knows."

"Oh, no!! She'll use this to get me. I'm so stupid. I can't live with her she's so mean!"

"Come on we have to face the music Carol," Rose insisted.

"Where is Emmett, Jenni? Has he left yet?" Barbara's not so dulcet tones rang out.

Emmett went to take the kids out to his patrol car through the front door but he overheard Barbara's voice in the front foyer and he decided to stop and listen in.

"Why are we stopping," asked Carol.

"Dad wants to overhear someone. Now stay quiet," Caleb whispered.

"Where's Emmett?" Barbara repeated, "I had some questions about the Banks/Crimshaw investigation."

"Oh, sorry, Ms. Hayes. I was dispatching some patrol cars. I think Emmett just left to take the kids home, but here's his latest filed reports. Kendall dropped them off," Jenni said offering some papers.

"Thanks Ms. Hayes," Barbara stated looking at the report, "Can I use you as a sound board?"

"Sure, I love to do some real police work."

"So we have another victim Grace-Ellen Singer? How does he connect to the investigation?" Barbara asked.

"As I understand it she's Harold Crimshaw's housekeeper."

"Hmm, that means she probably saw the killer and the killer knew it and got rid of her. This complicates things."

"Isn't it unusual for a Crown attorney to come into the picture at this point?"

"Can I tell you a secret Jenni? It's true Lily never did; but I'm not Lily and I don't want to be the Assistant Crown attorney forever; if I solve this crime and get a conviction maybe I could get to be the Crown Attorney in a place like Toronto or something. If some cop were to say help me and feed me more details then when I got to wherever I could be Crown attorney, I could put a good word in with the police department telling them all of that cop's help and they could get a better job," Barbara rattled off.

What was Barbara up to? She was never this assertive it seemed odd. Did she hide this side of herself only to have it come out now that Lily had to take time off? Emmett thought.

"Gee would you? I could get away from this desk and be an actual in the field cop. The sexist is rampant in this department. It's hard for a woman to get ahead," Jenni replied eagerly, "So if we figure out who killed them it's a win, win for both of us?"

"Exactly! Who is Emmett looking at for the crimes? Who has he interviewed?"

"Several people actually although he hasn't actually pegged anyone person for the crime." Jenni replied

"Has he looked at the family? Usually it's those closest to the person who does the killing," Barbara insisted.

"Chief Stewart had an alibi he was at his desk in full sight of cops here at the station. Terrence Stewart was getting married in London, Ontario. Audrey Stewart was on a private plane which arrived here at seven a.m. Cecilia Crimshaw has Alzheimer's disease. She has a caregiver 24 hours so she couldn't have done it," Jenni answered reading the paperwork.

"Hmm, likely story. Have they interviewed Cecilia's caregivers?"

"They interviewed one of them Geoffrey Harkness. He is a registered nurse. He said that he saw the squares in a green container when he took a break for ten minutes while Cecilia was sleeping in a chair. Harold offered him one saying he was on a diet tomorrow and that he didn't want sweets in the house after tonight. Geoffrey refused. Geoffrey said he doesn't like oranges or orange flavouring. The other caregiver at the time Roberta Santiago (the night lady) has left town and is being sought as a material witness," Jenni read.

"That's suspicious that she left town and hasn't been found. Any more leads that Emmett is working on?" Barbara inquired.

"The pest control guy, one Darby Henderson was spraying for pests the day before New Year's Eve. It seems that Harold was worried that he had brought home bed bugs in his luggage."

"Ooh, gross!"

"Well the pest control company Auntie Pesto's came out and sprayed. Everyone had to leave the house. Harold spent the day at City Hall. Cecilia went to an outpatient senior daycare program for the day. The staff was gone all day."

"Any chance the poison was not ginger but the bedbug poison?"

"No, the new coroner insists it was an anaphylactic reaction that killed both Harold and his daughter. The son-in-law was killed as a result of the car accident that was cause by his wife's reaction."

"I saw Harold at City Hall. He was working really hard on some initiatives he'd hope to bring in the New Year and he asked me to come and look at some legalities of them as a favour to him. Wait a minute. You said that Audrey Stewart was out of town. What were the dates she says she was out of town?"

"Let me see her alibi says she was gone from December 10 to January 1st."Jenni answered.

"Well isn't that interesting, considering I saw her at Harold's office two days before he was murdered. I'd say that bumps her up the list wouldn't you? And of course this Roberta Santiago as well," Barbara exclaimed.

"Wait until we solve this crime. Emmett thinks he's the expert since he lucked into to some solves last year." "Well a solve would go a long way to getting me that job and you too of course," Barbara insisted slyly.

Barbara was worse than he thought. She sounded like she was determined to make someone a scapegoat as long as it furthered her career. He wouldn't let her harm Lily's job. He'd already hurt Lily enough he couldn't let Barbara torpedo Lily's career too.

He better get the kids out of here before she spotted him and started grilling him. Emmett then herded Caleb, Rose and Carol out the back door of the police station and to his patrol car putting them in the back seat.

Driving them home to Katha's he heaved a sigh of relief. Caleb had done the right thing. He should be proud of him but Barbara sounded like she was gunning for Lily's job. Damn her! Lily worked hard for that job and he felt guilty because she was involved with him Sherry-Anne's troubles had gotten Lily shot. He had to work hard and make sure that Barbara didn't score points from this investigation that would harm Lily. He owed her that much!

~0~

Chapter 11 - Someone to Blame

The walls were all closing in and I felt trapped. They couldn't find out that I committed these murders; I had to give them a few red herrings, someone to blame this on other than myself of course. There must be someone out there who really deserved prison time. She couldn't find out what I had done it would kill her. She was such a goodie two shoes. I protected her just like I always did. This momentary lapse of hers could not be found out. She just wanted what everyone wanted… to love and be loved. What that so much to ask? I would protect that innocent spark in her. Everyone should be allowed their innocence. Unfortunately I had lost mine a long time ago. He entered our lives when we were young and I bared the scars as always to protect her.

She was so stressed these days running around like a whirlwind but she was really just tilting at windmills. No one cared about her not like I did. No one even knew her.

She was so alone eating her solitary dinners, night after night. I'd make this right for her. Then I'd find her someone nice who could take of her so I could rest. She was just so much work!!

But it would all end the way I wanted to. Someone more deserving would take the fall. And I would be free to live my life the way I chose to. Guarding, waiting, always protecting, her keeping her safe from harm.

~0~

Chapter 12 - Fallout

Lily's house

Emmett walked Rose and Carol to

Lily's door. Since Katha still isn't home; he knocked but no one answered. Rose then let them in the house with her key. Rose and Carol then ran upstairs. Lily is asleep on the sofa.

'Why Emmett what are you doing here?" Lily asked, as she grabbed together a ratty old blue housecoat at the neck to cover her top half.

"I'm sorry Lily for waking you. Obviously you need your rest. I can speak with Katha," Emmett rambled.

"Why are you here Emmett has something happened to Rose?" Lily demanded angrily

"I'm okay, mom. Caleb and I went to rescue Carol from this wild party and we were arrested," Rose blurted from the top of the stairs.

"Wild party? I assume Carol is up there with you? Get down here both of you."

Carol and Rose walked down the stairs at a slow pace like they were walking to their death.

"Carol do you have something to add to this?" Lily asked.

"I'm sorry; so sorry!! Please don't make Grandma Katha get rid of me," sobbed Carol.

"No one is getting rid of you honey we love you. You are family. Grandma Katha asked Amelia to be her daughter on paper; so she could hold onto you. Carol we love you," Lily stated trying to reassure Carol and then taking her in her arms in a bear hug.

"They'll hate me. I made Rose get arrested," Carol cried, almost incoherently.

"It's okay nothing you could do could make us hate you. Disappoint us; but hate you never," Lily stated.

"It was all my fault.......and (hiccup) all because I wanted to go out with that creep Bobby Bradford. He tried to...," Carol whined.

"Did he hurt you are you okay? I'll kill him if he hurt you," Lily asked outraged.

"No he didn't, but some guy ripped my shirt," Carol explained as Lily realized she hadn't noticed Carol was wearing a Happy Valley Police Department tee shirt

"You sure he didn't hurt you? You can tell me anything. I know it's not your fault," Lily pleaded.

"No, just ripped my shirt."

"Did you get this guy Emmett?" asked Lily outraged and angry

"No, we don't know who he is and Carol doesn't know his name," Emmett exclaimed.

"Please, Lily, I don't want to think about him or see him again." Carol insisted, "Can we just drop it?"

"I don't like it but if that's what you want."

"How did you get to Carol, Rose?"

"Caleb drove me there," Rose admitted.

"So I have your son to thank. I'm so glad he has the decency his father doesn't have. Tell Caleb I said thanks," Lily sniped.

"Can we talk Lily? Really talk?" Emmett pleaded.

"I don't think we have anything to talk about," Lily said tersely.

"Please Lily, I really miss you," Emmett continued to plea.

"I heard Sherry-Anne was living with you is that true?" Lily enquired.

"Yes, but it's only temporary and she and Caleb have their own rooms," Emmett admitted.

"Does she know it's temporary? No don't answer that."

"Do you miss me Lily? I miss you. I know I made a mistake; but it will never happen again," Emmett begged.

"Emmett maybe you should go."

"I'll go but I'm never giving up. I will win you back Lily," Emmett stated then he left.

Lily breathed a sigh of relief. She couldn't be around Emmett much longer. She might start crying or screaming, or begging him to take her back.

What the hell? She didn't want him back...she didn't!! He was a liar and a cheat and she didn't love him anymore, did she? No, she wouldn't care about him. It was good that he had left. Now she wouldn't have to see him.

"Wow he loves you; almost as much as Caleb loves me!" asked Rose stated beginning her plan.

"What did you say Rose?" Lily enquired ending up talking to Rose's back and getting no answer.

Lily wondered if she heard correctly surely Rose hadn't said that Caleb loves her unless she was talking about Caleb as a friend. Yes, that was it, no need to worry about Rose. She was just a nice kid who gathered friends like the flower she was. But still the looks between them lately maybe Lily should worry.

What a horrific night. First Barbara called to rub it in that she is doing Lily's job better than Lily ever did it, then Emmett came back into her life. God damn him. He was still living with that woman Sherry-Anne. He obviously cared about her. Why couldn't Emmett stay out of her business and away from Lily?

She knew she wasn't being fair. Emmett had saved the kids from having charges on their permanent records but it hurt to see him…

She had gone out on a few dates with Dr. Jones; but her heart hadn't been in them. Dafydd wanted to continue dating but Lily didn't think that was fair to him. Dafydd had convinced Lily however to give him another chance and she had to admit the man made her laugh.

Emmett had betrayed her in the worst way. He slept with a woman who was very like her; that's probably what hurt the most. Did he just go out with her as a substitute for Sherry-Anne?

Sherry-Anne had almost gotten Lily killed and then she had reached in and snatched back the man that Lily had wanted to marry. Emmett had proposed to Lily not Sherry-Anne so why had Sherry-Anne wound up with the prize? Why did Lily still long for Emmett? He was a cheat pure and simple. What was that old adage?

'Once a cheat always a cheat.' She wouldn't fall into that trap again. She'd thought she'd put those feelings behind her the last week but that all changed when she saw him as she awoke tonight. All she had wanted was for Emmett to take her in his arms and say that it was all a mistake that he loved her.

It hurt!! How it hurt that Sherry-Anne was living with him. And now was his son moving in on her little girl, Rose? Was it more than a friendship? The boy was seventeen years old far too old for an innocent fifteen year old girl like Rose. She had to put an end to this before it got worse; but if was mistaken and she told Rose that she couldn't see him or even date him then like any other teen Rose would do the opposite. So how could Lily handle this? She really needed to consult Grandma Katha. That woman was an expert planner heck let's just admit Grandma Katha was a master manipulator. Tomorrow she would consult Grandma Katha and make a plan everything would be okay.

Then there was Carol. Carol was feeling alone and unwanted they had to do more to make that poor child feel wanted. Maybe she'd speak to Rose about spending more time with her friend. Upstairs Carol and Rose were talking about Caleb.

"So you're dating Caleb and you didn't say a word? Some friend you are," Carol snarled.

"I'm sorry it just happened so fast you know?" Rose covered.

"No, I don't know because my best friend didn't say a word," Carol cried sounding hurt and angry.

"I'm sorry I should have said something sooner. You're right, you're my best friend. I can't keep this from you anymore," Rose stated.

"Keep what from me? Is there more to tell me? Did you sleep with him?" Carol asked, shrilly.

"Ooh yuck. Caleb and aren't really together we are pretending," Rose admitted.

"Why are you pretending to be dating?" Carol asked.

"It has nothing to do with you. Caleb and are pretending so we can get my mom and Emmett back together. Mom and Emmett are miserable without each other and if they had to talk about us dating they'd have to get together," Rose explained.

"Why would you do that? Emmett cheated on your mom with Caleb's mom."

"Did he or did she do something to him?"

"You think she drugged him?" Carol exclaimed.

"Yes, I do and so does Caleb." Rose stated, "But you have to keep this quiet for Caleb's sake."

"Harsh. I wouldn't put it past that witch. His own Mom did that? Poor Caleb, of course I won't say anything."

"Thank-you, Carol."

"I'm glad you finally decide to level with me. I guess we are friends after all."

"I'm glad too. It's too hard to keep things from my best friend. You're like my sister you know," Rose cried.

"You too. Now let me help you with this plan we can make it look really realistic and really alarm your mom. Then she'll have to talk to Emmett about how his so is too old for you. Yada, yada, yada!!" Carol answered, "I can tell Grandma Katha how worried I am about you. How you guys can't keep your hands off each other; that should get them both worried."

"You're the best person in the world Carol. Thanks again. Want to watch Blindside? I TiVoed it."

"You bet I just love strong female characters."

 "I love how strong Jane is," Rose stated.

"Do you think she's bad?" Carol asked

"No, she's had a hard life of it but she's trying to be good," Rose exclaimed

"Who do you think she'll end up with?" Carol enquired as they sit on the bed to watch.

"Darned if I know."

"Shush it's on." Rose stated.

"Like you're ever quiet!" Carol insisted and then dissolved into giggles that Rose answered with her own.

~0~

Chapter 13 - Barbara

T he damn kids were caught partying.

Where was the supervision for these children? Frankly Lily and Katha were falling down on the job. Lily was so perfect; it was nice to know she wasn't perfect at everything. Emmett who she admired was just as irresponsible at looking after his son. While okay maybe not just as responsible after all, that bitch Sherry-Anne Mobley had his kid and he had given them a stiff warning about their behaviour.

Barbara hadn't seen that bitch, Sherry-Anne in years. They'd gone to grade school together. Sherry-Anne had teased her unmercifully and had coached the other girls to bully her. Sherry-Anne was evil pure and simple. Oh she put on a good act of how she had been treated badly by her aunt and uncle but she knew what a slime ball Sherry-Anne was. Leopards didn't change their spots. Even Lily the good had experienced the wake of Sherry-Anne. Barbara had heard second-hand what had happened to Lily because of Sherry-Anne and her father. Of course Lily and her family did tend to attract tragedy so maybe it wasn't entirely Sherry-Anne's fault. Except it was…Barbara knew it was. Sherry-Anne was the devil; although it did benefit Barbara.

She wanted to do her job well. This was her chance with Lily out of the way. She had to find the mayor's killer and presented it in a way that she received all the credit. Lily would still retain her job when she was better but Barbara could move on to greener pastures. She could be a bright light in a place like Toronto.

She needed to lie in a bigger place where everyone was anonymous and didn't know everyone else's business like in Happy Valley. The name was a joke. She hadn't been happy a day she lived here.

She gone away to university and felt better
but then she had to return to look after her
elderly parents. First her mother had taken a
long painful journey through cancer to
death. Then she'd been left in the house with
him! Happy Valley might think they know
everyone's business but they didn't know
how her father had treated her. He had
abused her goodwill and made her stay at
home the last year as he lingered like the
evil do. Yet even death had gotten him in the
end he was gone and she was free. Free to
make her career count and move finally to a
big city. She had the last laugh on him
anyway he wanted to buried next to her
mother an she'd had him cremated and then
spread over a manure pile in the zoo.

She was done with him so why did he
continue haunting her? She wouldn't let him
ruin her life anymore. No she was taking her
life back. She would get to Toronto and she
would be a crown attorney there; then after
she became a star she quit that and open her
own practice and defend all those
millionaires that got in trouble there.

Maybe she'd even find a rich husband to go along with her career. She would have a happy life. She was determined.

~0~

Chapter 14 - Audrey

Katha's house

Katha crept out of bed and into the kitchen to make coffee. Terrence was in the shower and after all she just had to slip a couple of pods in the Tassimo and push a button and slip a cup under the nozzle. Terrence would do tit for her so why did she feel like she was letting down the entire female population because felt like she was acting like a man's version of a traditional wife? The doorbell rang interrupting her thoughts. It couldn't be Carol coming home from Lily's. Carol had a key, Katha thought. Who could be at the door this early? It was only six a.m. Katha wondered.

Katha opened the door to Audrey on her step.

"Good morning Audrey," Katha stated, remembering that as much as she disliked Audrey, Audrey was Terrence's daughter and therefore family.

Audrey didn't look like the Audrey Katha had ever seen. This Audrey looked like she slept in her clothes. Her hair hadn't been combed and her make-up was smeared on her face and hadn't been refreshed.

"Is my Dad here?" Audrey asked hesitantly.

"Are you okay Audrey?"

Audrey started crying as Katha ushered her in.

"Audrey please, stop crying and tell me what's wrong? How can I help?" Katha demanded.

"I need my Dad. He can help me! Daddy will save me. Is he here?" Audrey asked through tears.

"I'll get him. You sit right there and then you can tell us both what's wrong. You're family we will help you will fix whatever is wrong," Katha replied generously giving Audrey the coffee she'd just made and replenishing the water so she could make two more coffees.

"You'd do that for me? After all I have done… you know talking trash against you. And getting tons of money from daddy and then trying to take Carol from you?" Audrey asked drying her tears.

"Like I said Audrey, you are family. You are Terrence's daughter that makes me your step-mother. If you need help we will give it to you that is what family does," Katha stated

"I'm sorry I misjudged you Katha. I'd like to tell you what has happened. Maybe you can help me, but can I tell you and Dad this both at the same time?" Audrey asked.

"Yes, honey you just sit there and I'll go get Terrence,"

"Is the coffee ready, Katha?" asked Terrence suddenly appearing behind Katha and then noticing Audrey he exclaimed, "Oh Audrey I didn't see you there. Honey, what's wrong? Who has made my baby cry?"

"Daddy!!!" Audrey wailed.

"Stop your crying Audrey! Tell your father and me what is wrong, so we can fix it," Katha insisted.

Terrence looked at Katha in awe as Audrey responded.

"I did something stupid...,"Audrey started.

"What was that?" Terrence asked.

"I lied to the police," Audrey blurted.

"Hand me and your father a dollar each now," Katha demanded.

Audrey looked puzzled, but obeyed.

"Okay so this makes your Dad and me your lawyers anything you tell us we don't have to reveal to anyone. This makes it client, lawyer privilege," Katha stated.

"I don't understand."

"It protects you now, just tell us, Audrey. Katha and I will help you," Terrence stated.

"Oh… okay. I did go to Hawaii on December 10th, but I came home on December 28th, not January 1st, like I told the police," Audrey explained.

"How did you get someone to say you were on a private plane that arrived on January 1st?"Katha asked.

"My friend Nigel Bennington is a pilot and he covered for me. He did pick me up, but not in Hawaii. He picked me up in Toronto," Audrey exclaimed.

"When did you go to Toronto and what time did he pick you up in Toronto?" Katha demanded.

"I went on New Year's Eve day after I saw Harold," Audrey admitted.

"You saw Harold alive?" asked Terrence surprised.

"I saw Harold alive and I am so ashamed!" Audrey stumbled and then in a low almost whispering voice she said, "I did something horrible. I hope and pray you'll forgive me."

"Did you kill them?" Katha asked.

"No of course not. I wouldn't kill anyone but I had an affair with my sister's husband. Don't be mad at me, Daddy." she cried breaking off as she looked at her father.

"Your father is disappointed, but not mad. Are you Terrence?" Katha lead Terrence.

"No, of course I'm not mad. Katha's right we'll help you. Tell me what happened," Terrence begged as Katha smiled in approval.

"We broke it off some time ago. I knew it was wrong, but Harold called me that day he told me Cecilia needed to see me. I didn't know Cecilia had Alzheimer's but there's no excuse I slept with my sister's husband. When I got there Cecilia was nowhere to be seen and Harold grabbed me and tried to get me to sleep with him again. I thought he was going to rape me. I was so scared. I ran from him but he grabbed me again and I kicked him then we fought I smacked him and managed to leave. He was alive when I left; but if I tell them that they'll suspect me because that's a great motive," Audrey cried and then began pacing back and forth.

"What am I going to do? They're going to find out!" she wailed.

"We are going to handle this," Katha insisted then turning to Emmett she instructed, "Terrence call Emmett and tell him to get over here."

"Now sit down dear well I'll tell you what to say when Emmett gets here," Katha commanded.

"Why are you being so nice to me? I was so horrible to you. I'm sorry I won't go after Carol anymore," Audrey claimed.

"That's very mature of you," Katha stated, "Now sit, quit pacing and drink the coffee while I brief you."

"Emmett. Terrence Stewart here could you come over to our house? We have something to discuss with you. Yes, this is police business," Terrence says into his cell phone, "Thanks Emmett, see you soon."

"Emmett will be here in about a half an hour time enough to go over what you will say to him; though you could be in trouble for giving a false statement to the police. That is if they choose to pursue that," Terrence explained.

"I could go to jail!!" Audrey wailed.

"If it comes to that it's a misdemeanour. I'll plea you down to community service," Katha answered.

"I might have to pick up garbage or clean toilets?" Audrey complained.

"It's better than jail and who knows maybe it will teach you something. Katha's a damn good lawyer, almost better than me," Terrence insisted.

"But you were a judge."

"And Katha was a case winning defense lawyer."

"Good, because I think I need one. Thanks Katha, I really appreciate this," Audrey stated to Katha's surprise as they waited for Emmett.

Carol came in a few seconds later shaking the snow off her winter coat and removing her boots. She turned around and then entered the kitchen and saw Grandma Katha typing on her computer and Audrey sitting drinking coffee.

"What is she doing here? I know I was at that party. I'm not going to do that again. Don't make me go with her. Please, I'll do anything!!" Carol begged.

"Hey, I'm not here to take you. I've got my own problems," Audrey protested.

"What's this about a party? We will talk about this later young lady," Katha exclaimed.

"She didn't tell you? Ah, I have to get ready for school. Did you sign the permission form Rose and the rest of the class are going skiing at Heavenly Peak," Carol asked.

"Have you skied before Carol?" Katha enquired then fired off some more questions, "Do they require helmets? If they don't I still want you to wear one. Be careful of trees people die skiing into trees. If you hit your head you tell them to take you to a hospital immediately."

"I will Grandma Katha, I promise now will you sign the form? Please?" Carol begged.

"Rose is going then?"

"Lily already made her promise all the things you asked. Do you two get together about this stuff or what?"

"Do you need any money dear?" Katha inquired.

"Yes, thank you I thought I'd have to beg. I need the price of the trip and I could I have enough to buy lunch?"

"You never have to beg sweetie. I'm sorry. I'll start giving you a weekly allowance and of course any school trip monies. Here you are that should be enough."

"Must be nice to be a kid and not have to worry about anything," Audrey stated and then under her breath "And get plenty of money."

"Are you sure she's not going to take me?" Carol whispered to Katha as she pulled Katha away to the bottom of the stairs.

"I promise I will make sure she never takes you. Audrey wants me to do something for her and if she wants me to do it she'll sign a paper giving custody to me or your Great Uncle Edward, with Terrence us as secondary guardians. It will all be well not to worry my pet. You're safe and you're loved here," Katha insisted hugging Carol and kissing her on the cheek.

"I love too Grandma Katha," Carol answered.

"When I married Terrence you became my beloved great-granddaughter." Katha exclaimed, "Family means everything to me and mine. Never forget that you are family. Even cranky old Great-Aunt Audrey is family."

"She maybe family but she's pain thanks for handling her Grandma Katha. I have to get my ski sweater and then I'm heading out."

Carol then ran upstairs to retrieve her sweater and in less than five minutes had her coat and boots on.

"Got to go now or I'll be late for the bus," Carol exclaimed.

"Don't forget…"Katha shouted as Carol opened the front door.

"I know… helmets, one for me and one for Rose," Carol answered.

"Bye, dear, be safe and have fun."

Katha then turned back to Audrey, "Now Audrey, if I'm going to represent you then you need to make good on your promise to give custody of Carol to someone responsible. Here is a document that I just typed up on my computer in the kitchen. It basically says as you can read that you give up your suit and give full custody to Amelia or to Edward as the court chooses. Since your objections were that Terrence and are too old to raise her. We are however listed as secondary guardians."

"I guess I'll write in Edward then he has always been a good big brother to me," Audrey exclaimed then continued, "Are you sure that you can get me out of any jail time for lying to the police?"

Audrey then wrote Edward's name signed and dated in the places Katha indicated.

"It should be a piece of cake," Katha stated, "That is if you follow my lead."

"Where's Carol going?" Terrence asked absentmindedly.

"Carol's off on ski trip with her school," Katha answered.

"Skiing? Do you think that's a good idea? That's a dangerous sport. People get killed skiing. Look at that actress…"

"That's why I told her to be careful and wear a helmet." Katha says

"I guess we can't wrap her in cotton wool but I'd really like to."

"I know dear so would I but if we don't give them wings how can they fly?" Katha replied.

"That's why I love you, Katha. You think about everything and come up with the best solutions," Terrence answered.

"So you love me for my mind only?" Katha replied, sounding a little put out.

"No, I also love you for that heart that is as big as the ocean," Terrence answered, taking Katha in his arms and kissing her soundly.

"Ick, I'm sitting here waiting for the cops who could put me in jail. Don't you two ever knock it off? My life is on the line here and you are both too old to be necking," Audrey sniped.

The doorbell rang; Audrey shivered and stiffened in anticipation. Then she stared to pace and shake slightly. Terence put his arm around his daughter and got her to sit down. Katha then opened the door to a snow covered Emmett.

"Emmett, come in it's really blowing out there," Katha said sweetly, "Come in and have some coffee and biscuits after you take off your boots and coat."

"I came as soon as I could is something up with Terrence or Lily?"

"It's Audrey."

"Audrey? You're civil to her? But I thought she was trying to take Carol from you two," Emmett exclaimed.

"Not anymore she's signed over Carol to Edward. She's our family she's here and she wants to talk to you. I'm representing her as her lawyer," Katha stated.

"Take me to her."

Emmett walked into the kitchen and sat in the only open chair.

"Ms. Stewart what can I do for you?" Emmett asked as Katha prodded Audrey.

"I lied," Audrey whimpered.

"What was that?"

"I lied… okay I lied!!" Audrey shouted.

"You lied about what Ms. Stewart?" Emmett demanded removing his notebook and taking notes.

"My statement which I gave to the police was a lie," Audrey answered.

"Could you clarify that Ms. Stewart? What part of your statement was a lie?" Emmett demanded.

"Um… I did go to Hawaii on December 10th, but I came home on December 28th not January 1st like I told the police," Audrey admitted.

"Testimony from one Nigel Bennington said he picked you up in Hawaii," Emmett exclaimed.

"He won't get in trouble will he? I made him cover for me. He picked me up in Toronto," Audrey stated.

"When did you get back from Hawaii? We have confirmation that you arrived there December 10th," Emmett claimed.

Audrey looked to Katha for courage and when Katha nodded she said, "I got in to Happy Valley about seven p.m. December 28th."

"Okay, so when did you leave for Toronto where Mr. Bennington picked you up?"

"I went on New Year's Eve day after I saw Harold…," Audrey admitted.

"You saw Harold alive? "Emmett asked excited.

Audrey looked at Katha who nodded again.

"Yes, but it was the day before New Year's Eve, December 30th,"Audrey explained.

"And why did you go there?"

"I didn't know about Cecilia's illness, Harold called me. He said my sister Cecilia wanted to see me, but he lied. He just wanted to hook-up," Audrey stated blushing.

"Why would he have done that?"

"I had an affair with Harold but I broke it off with him," Audrey stated looking contrite and embarrassed.

"I see and how long did this affair take place?" Emmett asked softly.

"Three years, off and on .I ...."Audrey whispered.

"You what? Ms. Stewart what were you going to say?"

"Harold was supplying drugs to me in exchange for sex."

"How long did that take place from what date to what date?"

"I had an affair from January four years ago to January a year ago," Audrey answered.

"And where did you get your drugs after you broke up?"

"Do I have to answer that?" Audrey asked Katha.

"My client refuses to answer that on the grounds it could incriminate her," Katha stated.

"So are you still an addict, Ms. Stewart?"

"No, I went to rehabilitation here but I relapsed and my friend Nigel paid for my trip to Hawaii. He has a friend there who runs a rehab. I spent a couple of weeks in his rehab clinic and I'm clean now," Audrey answered.

"So what happened when you refused to have sex with Mr. Crimshaw?"

"I told him it was over a long time ago that I was clean and he said he could change all that all he had to do was slip something in my drink."

"So you gave him some orange ginger squares?"

"No way!! I didn't kill him. I admit I smacked him and left, but he was alive when I left. Then my friend Liz called me and said New Year's was not a time for an addict to be home alone so I flew to Toronto that night and then flew home New Year's Day," Audrey exclaimed.

"May I have Liz's full name and her address? I'd also like a recent number for Mr. Bennington the number he gave us is not in order," Emmett queried.

Audrey wrote down the addresses and phone numbers on a paper supplied by Katha and handed the paper over to Emmett.

"Is everything okay now? I'm sorry I lied I didn't want anyone to find out I was an addict and that I had trade sex for drugs," Audrey insisted.

"What you did is a crime, lying to the police and giving false statements but since you came forward on your own before we found out on our own I think we can let it go" Emmett says "but don't let it happen again."

"Oh thank God. I'm not going to jail." Audrey replied, relieved.

"As long as you didn't kill Harold, that is! You do have one hell of a motive."

"I didn't, I didn't kill Harold!! He was pain in the ass, but Cecilia loved him," Audrey stated.

"I have my eye on you Ms. Stewart and if you committed this crime you will pay. Don't leave town," Emmett stated went to the front door to leave. His cell phone rang and he answered it as he went to go out the front door.

"Hello Barbara. Yes, uh, huh. Actually Ms. Stewart already cleared that up. No, we won't be arresting her at this time. We have no evidence linking her to the crime. Yes, we will be keeping her on the suspect list. Yes, I will be filling out a complete report. Goodbye Barbara," Emmett said then hung up his cell phone.

"Stay on the right side of the law, Ms. Stewart."

"I will I promise," Audrey insisted.

Emmett then left. Audrey let out a sigh of relief and Terrence offered to set his daughter up in an apartment he owned and pay her rent until she could get on her feet. Katha thought that was going a little far but she wouldn't have done the same for Amelia or Lily so who was she to quibble.

Happy Valley Police Station

Emmett entered the police station shaking off the snow that had gathered on his coat and boots. He was thinking about what Audrey had revealed. She should be higher on the suspect list but his gut was telling him that Audrey hadn't killed Harold. He hoped his gut wasn't wrong because Katha and Terrence have a vested interest in Audrey and he wouldn't hurt them for the world. He was just glad that Katha was still speaking to him after what he done to Lily.

The weather was getting positively nasty outside. He heard on the radio they were expecting a snowstorm. Surely Happy Valley High School really wasn't still going ahead with the ski trip he overheard Carol mention. Come to think of it Caleb said he was going on the same trip. He should find out if the trip had been cancelled. He really wasn't comfortable with the kids going skiing in this weather they'd probably have an accident or something.

Emmett dialed the office of Happy Valley High School.

"This is Sergeant Detective Emmett Rogers of the Happy Valley police force. Uh huh, no it's nothing too serious. I'm just inquiring about the ski trip that was to take place today to Heavenly Peak. Uh huh, not until tomorrow? Could you do one more thing for me could you check if Caleb Rogers, Carol Banks and Rose Brooksfield are in class?" Emmett pleaded.

Emmett heard it but couldn't believe it they'd skipped class all three of them and lied to their guardians about it.

"Where were they?" Emmett wondered. He'd have to look for them on his break. He couldn't get away until about two hours from now for lunch as he was late as it was for a meeting with the chief. Emmett headed for his desk to pick up messages.

"Morning Emmett, you're late partner. I covered for you with the chief," Kendall said seeing Emmett

"Good morning Kendall," Emmett says "Thanks for covering for me. I was taking a statement it seems that Audrey Stewart lied and wanted to retract her statement and give a true statement. She moves a little higher on the suspect list but my gut feeling is she didn't do it."

"Sounds like you've been busy chasing down leads. So have I."

"What do you have?" Emmett inquired still thinking about the kids and a little distracted.

"I have a new suspect. My suspect had an affair with the victim that resulted in a child," Kendall gloated.

"Really? Who is she?"

"Someone we both know but apparently not as well as we thought." Kendall stated cryptically.

"Quit keeping me in suspense Kendall just tell me who it is!"

"Brandy Calders," Kendall exclaimed, smugly.

"When did she have Harold Crimshaw's child?" Emmett blurted.

"That's the thing no one even knew she was pregnant until she went on maternity leave and told her supervisor," Kendall stated.

"Kendall you are not answering the question. When did she have the child?"

"She had a child, a little girl she called Harriet Robin, at Hallowe'en to be exact." Kendall says "She put Harold's name on the birth certificate."

"But she didn't even look pregnant just a little over weight," Emmett exclaimed, "And she was sniffing around that serial killer Brad Owens back in June. It doesn't add up."

"Oh it adds up partner. She broke up with Harold back in February right after she told him she was pregnant. She had a knock down drag out fight with him and was ejected from City Hall over it. She was angry he was denying her child. She has motive to spare and no alibi," Kendall claimed.

"A lot of people have no alibis and motive we have to dig deeper partner and prove who did it."

"So where do we go from here?" Kendall asked.

"We have to find what those squares were in. They had to be in something at Harold's."

"Maybe the dish was washed?"

"Could be? Although what was Francine carrying her squares in?" Emmett enquired.

"Serviettes? I don't know," Kendall exclaimed, frustrated.

"That's what we need to find out partner. Was anything found in the car?"

"No, nothing but serviettes in the car," Kendall stated.

"They had to be in something. Francine was a bit of a neat freak she wouldn't have had them just in napkins," Emmett insisted.

"Nothing found partner. What do you suggest we do?"

"We should interview Brandy but first I want to take a trip over to city hall and talk to the security guard. They're very observant they sign people in every day maybe one of the guards saw the container the squares were in if they were given to Harold at the office?" Emmett queried.

"Yes, good thinking partner let's head over to City Hall. Maybe we can get the proof to nail Brandy while we are there and then we can wrap this up in a tidy little bow."

"One can only hope," Emmett replied.

~0~

Chapter 15 – Skipping School

Early this morning

Carol felt a little guilty for deceiving Grandma Katha but somehow she didn't think Grandma Katha would approve of her skipping school even for such a good cause. She'd called Rose and Caleb before she left and they were willing to help. She had to go to the place her Mom and Dad had died. Her mother's insistence in her dream last night had decided her. She felt her Mom and Dad and grandfather really could be at rest until they discovered the murderer. Mom was insisting in the dream that she could find a clue to the murderer where they died.

She was quite sure what she would be looking for; but Caleb and Rose could help her. Caleb being able to drive them to the site would really help. Good they're she had to get in quickly before Emmett saw them. He wouldn't like it but she had to do this.

"Get in so here are the notes I forged for school. We should be able to go out there and look around and get back to school by lunch," Caleb exclaimed.

"This had better be worth it. I've never skipped school before," Rose stated looking worried.

"I have to look. You know I do. My mom keeps coming into my dreams telling me to look," Carol stated.

"Sorry for complaining we will look. Do you have any idea what we are looking for?" Rose asked.

"I'm not sure, but I'm thinking she was killed by a square so maybe the container? What do you think?" Carol enquired.

"I think that's a great idea," Caleb answered.

"Me too," Rose exclaimed.

"This weather is getting worse I hope we can find anything in this snow," Caleb stated, "There wasn't this much snow when they had their accident was there?"

"No, there wasn't, but I still want to look," Carol insisted.

"Okay, but we have to hurry. I heard on the radio just before I picked you both up that there is a snowstorm coming. We're going to get 15 centimetres," Caleb countered.

"Oh, so that is what Grandma Katha meant when she said 6 inches. I didn't have a clue what she was talking about," Carol cried.

"Grandma Katha says they weren't taught the metric system in school and she finds it hard to convert it all the time. I said why bother? Then she said wait until you get older everything changes," Rose explained.

"We're here. Let's park the car over there and start looking," Caleb stated.

Caleb, Rose and Carol looked around at the site where the accident occurred. There was a huge culvert beside the road and a small cliff where the snow lay heavy and dipped down into a culvert.

"We can't go down that cliff it will kill us," Caleb insisted.

"Maybe it didn't go down there .The impact would have thrown their car into the oncoming car. So maybe it's over there?" Carol cried pointing to the opposite side of the road where there is a small dip beside the road.

"I don't know how we can find anything in this snow," complained Caleb.

"I'm getting cold can we come back another day Carol?" Rose begged.

"Give me another twenty-five minutes and if we don't find anything will go and get hot chocolate my treat." pleaded Carol.

"Fine, but it's really cold and my toes are becoming popsicles here," Rose complained.

"You should have worn warmer boots. You said you were going skiing, remember? Some friend you are a little snow and you wuss out," Carol sniped.

Carol then glared at Rose. Caleb thought he'd have to break up a fight between the two girls when he spotted something.

"What is that?" Caleb asked.

"I think it's a container. Do you think we found it?" Carol exclaimed.

"Don't touch it with your bare hand. I have a plastic glove here. Let me get it. I have a plastic evidence bag," Caleb cried excited.

"Where did you get them?" Carol asked.

"I kind of borrowed them from my Dad's kit. I hope he doesn't notice they are missing or I'm going to be in deep trouble," Caleb stated.

"Me too still but when you give him the evidence won't he know?" Rose asked.

"Yes, I guess.so I'm going to be in trouble anyway," Caleb answered.

"Wait a minute, I brought a camera to prove this is where we found the evidence," Carol replied, "Let's take a picture first before we dig it out and before we touch it."

"Okay, but hurry up. I think I'm getting frostbite," Rose complained.

Carol took a picture with the camera she brought then she turned and took the card out of the camera and slipped it in her pocket.

"Got it and it's in the evidence bag," Caleb insisted.

"I don't think so. Hand it over kids," a woman's voice said.

When the kids looked up they noticed she was directly in their path dressed in a blue parka her right hand held a pistol pointed directly at them.

~0~

Chapter 16 - Curiosity

Katha knitted while sitting in her living

room chair. Terrence stood at the window watching the snow come down and looked pensive.

"Wow it's really coming down out there," Terrence stated.

"Have you heard a word I have said Terrence?" Katha asked.

"Did you say something dear?" Terrence asked, distracted.

"I said a lot of somethings. I was talking about the fact that they haven't caught the murder yet, but that even though your daughter Audrey was a bit of a brat; she didn't do it." Katha stated.

"I know she's spoiled and that is my fault. When her mother and I split she was so little and I felt so guilty that I spoiled her. I know what you're thinking spare the rod and spoil the child," Terrence answered, "But I'm glad you can see there is some good in my daughter."

"Terrence, she had you as her father, she can't be all bad," Katha insisted.

"Thanks honey for being there for my girl and helping her out when she lied to the police," Terrence exclaimed.

"She'll be okay. We'll be there when and if she needs us," Katha cried, "Meanwhile we have to figure out some other suspects for them."

"I used to visit Cecilia a lot; but since she stopped remembering who I was, I've gone a lot less," Terrence explained.

"I seem to remember Harold having a notebook that he kept as his personal diary/planner. Where do you think that is?" Katha asked.

"The police would have their suspect by now if they found it."

"I wonder if they checked his secret cubbyhole?" Katha enquired.

"Secret cubbyhole? How do you know about any secret cubbyhole?" Terrence wondered.

"I went to see Harold about some hospital business and his secretary had stepped away from her desk so I knocked then entered his office. He was bent over his desk upside down and as I observed he triggered a secret drawer in which he placed a small notebook."

"And then what happened? Did he see you?" Terrence excitedly enquired.

"No. I backed out of the room and knocked loudly on the door I closed again. Harold came to the door and opened it."

"We should go see if it's still there," Terrence insisted.

"Are you that bored?"

"Yes, I am bored, but if it will clear Audrey that would be a bonus."

"Okay but I'm not sure how will get past the guard," Katha exclaimed.

"That won't a problem my dear. I believe my cousin's boy is working there to put himself through college. I offered to pay for him, but the boy is so proud. I arranged for some grants and allowed him to pay for his basic needs; through a job I got him at City Hall. I mean anyone who wants to start all over and get an education at forty should get a hand," Terrence admitted.

"What is his name dear? Have I met him?" Katha wondered.

"His name is Barney Terrell. Actually his daughter is working for Amelia. Her name is Susan. Susan is taking night and on-line courses she wants a university degree too," Terrence explained.

"What? That creepy man is your cousin's son?"

"Creepy? I admit that Barney can be a little socially awkward, but he's a good guy."

"Dear you really have to tell me more about your family even the distant ones. It seems we keep running into your family without me being aware of who they are," Katha replied.

"So do you want to go off to City Hall to explore Harold's secret hiding place?" Terrence asked.

"Yes, dear; but first I have to make a couple of calls to set up a baby shower."

"For whom? Who had a baby?" Terrence asked, puzzled.

"Not a baby, she had two babies. She had two beautiful sweet little girls," Katha exclaimed.

"One of our relatives? Katha tell me who had the babies?" Terrence exclaimed, getting frustrated.

"No, Emmett's sister, Suzy Rogers," Katha answered.

"Oh that poor child. How big were the babies?" Terrence asked.

"They were 5 pounds and 6 pounds. They are very healthy little girls born about three weeks ago," Katha explained.

"If they were born three weeks ago why are you having a shower for them now?" Terrence asked.

"Suzy was in the hospital long before the babies were born, so we didn't want to have a shower then. So I waited a little while for her to get used to having two babies around," Katha stated.

"I know what you're up to old gal and it has nothing to do with those two babies. You want Lily to be happy again so you're finding a way to get them to see each other. Are you sure this is a good idea? He cheated on her with another woman who looked like her," Terrence answered.

"I think there's something weird going on there and I'd like to get to the bottom of it. You know I researched on the internet and there are drugs that people can get that can make them do that and not know what happened. I'm sure you heard about them in your practice as well."

"Roofies? You're thinking that witch slipped Emmett Rohypnol?" Terrence demanded.

"I'm wondering, but I have no proof and the proof is probably gone by now," Katha stated.

"There's more than one way to get to this problem. You work on your baby shower and getting those two in the same room. They have both sex baby showers now don't they? So you can invite both men and women and they can't refuse because then they'll look like heels," Terrence enquired.

"That was the plan."

"I like the way you think Katha," Terrence exclaimed.

"I'm ready to go now the baby shower plans are in place. I invited the witch"

"Why would you invite her?"

"I felt I had to. Do you think you can take her aside there and get her to confess?" Katha asked.

"My darling Katha I was a judge for many years. I know how to get criminals to confess," Terrence insisted; "Let me just check the mail he post person has been."

Terrence checked the mail and found an official city letter in the box.

"What in the hell is this? Do you know, Katha?"

"Oh crap they've gone and done it, haven't they?"

Terrence alarmed opens the envelope.

"They're expropriating our house and land for the rapid transit street widening," Terrence cried angrily.

"Damn it! I've been trying to get them to change the route this means they're expropriating Lily's property too and since Amelia lives on that property too then we're are out of a home." Katha exclaimed, "What are we going to do?"

"I have plenty of money. I'll solve this problem. I can contact a real estate person later today but for now we should cool down and look into that book,"

"So are we off to City Hall?" Katha asked.

"Yes, I want a look at that book and to give that council a piece of my mind for taking our homes," Terrence stated.

"Keep your temper dear. I wouldn't want Emmett took come and arrest you," Katha exclaimed.

"I'll try, let's find that small notebook."

~0~

Chapter 17 - Brandy

Emmett and Kendall arrived at Brandy Calder's home and Emmett wrapped loudly on the front door. A bedraggled Brandy opened the door. Her red gold hair was now unkempt and flat and she wore stained sweatpants and a milk-stained sweatshirt. Her eyes were deeply shadowed as she held a screaming baby is on her shoulder.

"Come in quickly before my little girl, Harriet Robin gets cold .She's already unhappy today. I think maybe she's getting a first tooth," Brandy exclaimed.

"A little soon for that tooth aren't you still breastfeeding?" Kendall asked.

Emmett shot Kendall a disapproving look.

"We're sorry for interrupting your day. I'm sure it's difficult to be a sole parent," Emmett sympathized.

"Come in and set your coats on that chair," Brandy stated briskly.

Kendall and Emmett walked in and took off their coats and boots.

"Please sit down. I guess you didn't know I was pregnant most of my colleagues didn't. You probably thought I was just fat."

"I didn't really think about it. Not very observant for a cop am I?" Emmett admitted.

"Emmett you're just sweet that's all," Brandy flirted.

"That's really nice of you, but Brandy we need to talk to you," Emmett insisted.

"Me? What would you have to talk to me about?"

"How about we talk to you about the father of your child?" Kendall demanded.

"The father? Harriet's father? That's really none of your business .He's dead… that's all you have to know."

"We know Harriet Robin's father was murdered," Kendall stated.

"What are you talking about? It was an allergic reaction."

"Someone poisoned Harold Crimshaw? Was that person you?" Kendall asked.

"Me, you suspect me?"

"Why not you're a CSI tech you have the skills and you were involved with Harold. You have his daughter and he wasn't there for either of you," Kendall continued forcefully.

"Emmett, please don't let her railroad me. I admit I was involved with a married man. He strung me along, said he'd divorce his wife, but when he denied that I could ever be his wife even while I told him I was pregnant while that was the end for me. I moved on and decide to raise my child myself. Silly me! I did reach out to another man who turned out to be helping a serial killer. You all know about Silas Rentford. Then Silas was killed. I'm very unlucky when it comes to love, but I'm no killer. Frankly I don't have any time with Harriet Robin; when could I have killed Harold?" Brandy stated.

"I'm inclined to believe her Kendall," Emmett admitted.

"She does have a ring of truth to her story," Kendall admitted.

"So you believe me?"

"Maybe," Kendall stated not sounding sure.

"What would convince you? Maybe if I told you some of the names of Harold's women? You should be looking at that."

"Go ahead," Emmett stated "Tell us some names if the women you know of who were with Harold."

"Harold had something going on with Audrey Stewart. He tried to tell me it was just business but I caught them in bed when I went to tell him I was pregnant," Brandy explained.

"We already knew about Ms. Stewart .We don't think she was responsible." Kendall insisted.

"I don't know who else I can give you. I mean I saw someone with him but he said it was business and it could have been," Brandy hesitantly stated, "It was someone he saw all the time whose office is at City Hall. Someone who he thought could really help him."

"Who was this?" Emmett asked his eyes narrowing.

Brandy looked at Kendall as if she doesn't trust her and whispers the answer into Emmett's ear

"You saw them together in what way?" Emmett asked looking shocked.

"I saw her kiss him full on the lips then he took her hand and took her into his bedroom I left before either of them saw me," Brandy admitted.

"You've been a big help Brandy. Don't discuss this with anyone and just maybe you can help us catch this ruthless killer," Emmett stated.

Emmett and Kendall then said their goodbyes as they put their coats and boots back on.

"So how are Suzy and the twins? She must be overwhelmed with two new babies," Kendall asked as they walked to the patrol car.

"Suzy and the girls are okay. They're staying at my house for a few weeks until Suzy gets her strength back," Emmett exclaimed.

"I bet Sherry-Anne doesn't like that," Kendall commented.

"Sherry-Anne is getting on my last nerve. She keeps complaining about the babies crying. I told her that she needs to start looking harder for her own place."

"Your too easy on her .find her a place and move her into or you'll never get rid of her," Kendall stated.

"You might be right but I still want my son in my life," Emmett admitted.

"You are just too nice she's walking all over you Emmett. I think I prefer Lily over Sherry-Anne. Do you know what she told me when you stopped off to pick up something the other day?"

"What did she say?" Emmett asks getting in the passenger side of the patrol car

"She said that I was to keep my manicured hands off her man," Kendall stated "The nerve of that woman you are my partner nothing more. Did she speak that way to Lily?"

"Hmm," Emmett muttered.

Kendall was right Sherry-Anne had to go. Then maybe he could make some headway with Lily as well. Emmett thought. The longer she stayed the less chance of Lily ever forgiving him.

Emmett started thinking about the fact the kids aren't in school. Where could they be? Carol and Rose had bungled into the last murders and this one was probably no different.

Could it be that they were searching for clues themselves? If he were Carol, where would he search? The place where the accident took place… the container? Of course! He had to get to City Hall and seek some new evidence on their new suspect first, but he could call in a favour and get Alan Barnes to swing by and see if the kids were there.

"Alan, Emmett here. Could you do me a favour and swing by Elizabeth Canyon and Edward Street. Yes, the Banks' accident site. See if my son Caleb Rogers, Carol Banks and Rose Brooksfield are there. My son is driving a 1985 blue Mercury Topaz. Thanks, Alan, I owe you one."

"What was that about Emmett?" Kendall asks driving the patrol car, "It's a school day are they playing hooky and investigating our case?"

"It would seem so. I'm afraid they may be playing cop." "I hope not," Kendall exclaimed.

"That's why I sent Alan to find them," Emmett stated.

"So we are on the same page. You're thinking that she could have committed the murders too?"

"Definitely after that conversation we had with Brandy."

"We should arrest her now."

"No we need more evidence and I think we may be able to find it at City Hall."

"Good thinking partner now let's go find us some evidence at City hall to tie her in to this murder," Kendall replied.

"I hope we can then we can get the children to relax. They really shouldn't be looking into police matters."

"No they shouldn't, because I'm pretty sure this killer has no remorse. The killer wouldn't think twice about killing some kids.

~0~

Chapter 18 – Not Again

Carol, Caleb and Rose at the accident site where Carol's parents died have found a container, which they believe the murderer transplanted the squares in.

"Wait a minute, I brought a camera to prove this is where we found the evidence," Carol replied, "Let's take a picture first before we dig it out and before we touch it."

"Okay, but hurry up. I think I'm getting frostbite," Rose complained.

Carol took a picture with the camera she brought then she turned and took the card out of the camera and slipped it in her pocket.

"Got it and it's in the evidence bag," Caleb insisted.

"I don't think so. Hand it over kids," a woman's voice said.

When the kids looked up they noticed she was directly in their path dressed in a blue parka her right hand held a pistol pointed directly at them.

A woman looked on at the scene in dismay. Why did they have to find the container? She thought. All that searching I had done for her and now Carol is the one that finds that damn container. Then she has to panic and pull out a gun on children? How do I pull her fat out of this one? How do I explain the gun? How did she figure out about Harold and the squares anyway? I killed that evil cretin, not her. Yet somehow she had become aware of the crime and thought it hers. I was slipping up, she was becoming too self-aware.

This wouldn't do; but how to get out of this, without harming the children? The children were not too be armed at all costs. Carol had already suffered. She couldn't be allowed to cause the child more pain.

Did I really think this would be easy? She always got herself in messes; but this was the biggest one yet. If I didn't handle this correctly the children would become collateral damage. However I always have a back-up plan and the ropes plus the plastic zip ties; I found in her trunk would be my back-up plan.

"Sorry to scare you kids with the gun. I forgot I had it out. I got scared a couple of minutes ago by a bear. Must be that global warming they're always talking about bringing the bears down so far and closer to civilization."

"I heard polar bears were seen in Winnipeg," Rose pretended.

"Yes, I heard that too," Carol agreed picking up Rose clues to agree with everything Rose said.

"What the hell is wrong with you, two? The woman didn't see a bear she pulled a gun on us because she killed them. She made the squares .That's her container and you're giving the evidence to her?" Caleb replied angrily, "What about your parents, your grandfather? She murdered them."

"You're an idiot Caleb there are bears here. I've seen them," Rose said through clenched teeth.

"Damn you, Caleb Rogers. Why did you have to be so like your father? Rose and Carol believed me .You just had to question now where did it get you, Caleb Rogers? You and your friends will just have to do what I say now. I have the gun. Now you use this and tie up the girl's hands." she said holding out plastic ties.

"I won't."

"You will or I'll just shoot one of them. Now which one do you want me to shoot Caleb?" She said forcefully.

"Fine! Give me the rope. You should just keep me and let the girls go. You know my Dad he'll negotiate with you," Caleb exclaimed.

"We are going to put the girls in my trunk just for a little while. If you cooperate they won't be hurt," she replied calmly.

"Please don't do this," Caleb begged.

"It won't harm them. I promise."

Caleb tied up the two girls saying "Sorry."

The woman then placed both girls in a trunk of an older model car nearby.

"And what will you do with me?" Caleb asked.

"You turn around, "she said as he complied and she tied his hands with rope behind his back.

"What are you going to do to me?" Caleb asked again sounding frightened.

In answer she popped the trunk of Caleb's car and told him as she shut the trunk, "I'm so sorry Caleb I really am. You are a nice boy and I am fond of Emmett, but you really shouldn't have bumbled into this. You can't fit in the same trunk as the girls."

Caleb heard as the trunk lid shut, "I have to go now. I'll leave it to fate what happened to the both of us. Should you not be found before you freeze to death well then I win… or maybe it is lose since I must then take the life of these nice little girls. Goodbye Caleb."

Caleb waited a few minutes and then began kicking at the trunk trying to get free. He hit out with his right foot but it didn't work he tried to move in the trunk to get his hands near the wires that opened the trunk but it was impossible.

Caleb thought about all the things he hadn't done in life and how it was all going to end like this and then he struggled some more. There had to be a way to get out of this predicament after all it wasn't only his life at stake but Rose and Carol's too. And it seemed that only the three of them knew who the murderess was. He couldn't let her kill them all. He had to break free…somehow.

~0~

Chapter 19 - Guilt isn't eating me alive!!

Happy Valley Hospital

Sherry-Anne had just finished a twelve hour shift as a nurse and breathed a sigh it had been a long shift and she was so tired. She just wasn't getting enough sleep. Those twin babies of Suzy's were cute; but they kept her awake when she should be sleeping during the day working these night shifts. She probably had three hours of sleep yesterday. This wouldn't do especially with the new life growing within her.

Sherry-Anne felt incredibly guilty how she had tricked Emmett into sleeping with her. Poor Emmet all he had done sleep in the same bed with her.

When she had heard Lily's click in the lock Sherry-Anne had seen her chance to make them both believe that Emmett had slept with her. Now the months had gone by and Sherry-Anne felt empty and guilty. She was so afraid that Emmett would find out what she had done; then instead of enjoying the birth of her baby she'd be having the baby in jail.

Sherry-Anne knew she hadn't been in her right mind but that wasn't a good enough excuse for what she had done. Thinking of the baby growing in her womb and what a wonderful father Emmett would be for that baby was a great thing, but tricking him by drugging him she knew she deserved to be punished. It wasn't fair to either the baby or Emmett if she continued this ruse. Yes, a little part of her wanted the teenage Emmett back…the boy she had fallen in love with so long ago. How she long to go back and undue what she had done. Not that she regretted this child she loved this child, but she wished that this baby really was Emmett's instead of some stranger she been so attracted to that she broke her rule slipped into bed with him and created this new life.

That Christmas party in early December had been an awakening of Sherry-Anne. She met a charming visiting doctor who had awakened the girl that Sherry-Anne once was. He was so good looking. I mean who wouldn't be interested in a man that looked like a young Pierce Brosnan.

Sherry-Anne had a few too many drinks and the next thing she remembered she awoke in a bed with that young looking Pierce Brosnan sleeping beside her.

She gathered her clothes and left. A few days she became as regular as clockwork had not come. She took one of the earliest pregnancy tests and found to her dismay, then joy that she was pregnant. She didn't know the baby's father's name let alone where he lived. She became scared and depressed and Caleb became worried about her. She'd passed it off as a cold so Caleb wouldn't worry and then Caleb had found Emmett.

Emmett the only man she had ever loved. It was like fate was giving her back what she should have had when Caleb was a baby. Then she had seen the obstacle Lily.

Lily was everything she was not and Sherry-Anne was scared that Emmett was slipping from her grasp so she had concocted a wild plan to get Emmett to choose her. And it had gone even better than she had planned.

Sherry-Anne was ashamed. She had felt like a whore. She didn't sleep with strangers. She knew that times had changed women could do what they pleased but that wasn't her. She slept with two men in her life and both times she had become pregnant. She was also starting to think that her vision of Emmett might be skewed. He wasn't the same person she'd fallen in love with all those years ago. He had fallen in love with that woman Lily Brooksfield or Kelly, or whatever the hell last name *she* called herself. Sherry-Anne was seeing how miserable Emmett was without that woman and it was tearing Sherry-Anne apart. No she wouldn't feel that guilty. Guilt wouldn't eat her alive and yet she knew it was.

Sherry-Anne knew that what she had done was beyond wrong, it was criminal. She couldn't live with herself anymore. She hadn't been able to tell Emmett about her baby, the fact that it wasn't his. She had to tell Emmett the truth and if he chose to go back to Lily then at least one of them would be happy. She only hoped that one day Emmett would forgive her because if it didn't it would kill her. Sherry-Anne so deep in thought barely heard a man come up to her and ask, "Sherry-Anne is that really you?"

Sherry-Anne turned around in amazement. *It is him!*

The father of her baby maybe the universe was trying to tell her something. She looked at him, he was so incredibly good looking and he had been so kind to her that night. She felt her heart begin to beat a little faster and a rosy glow come over her. She did still have an attraction to him!!

"I can't believe I ran into you here of all places. You disappeared completely. I looked for you," Doctor Dafydd Jones exclaimed.

"I was scared," Sherry-Anne answered.

"I know me too. I tried to move on with another woman but she wasn't you. The night we met was kismet. I know it sounds ridiculous but it felt like fate that you came into my life and now it's throwing you back into my life again," Dafydd admitted.

Sherry-Anne smiled.

"Do you work here?"

"Yes, I just finished my shift," Sherry-Anne admitted.

"Come to breakfast with me?" Dafydd pleaded, "Please?"

"I'd like that," Sherry-Anne replied smiling at him again.

Sherry-Anne and Dafydd went to the Break an Egg Restaurant next to the hospital. Sherry-Anne ordered the big breakfast and Dafydd surprised her by ordering the same thing. While they waited the waitress poured coffee for both of them and they chatted while drinking it.

"So do you live her now?" Dafydd asked.

"I moved here in January. Is this where you live?" Sherry-Anne replied.

"Yes, I live her now. I took up a position at the hospital, here, in January. You haven't said my name have you forgot it?" Dafydd asked and then said gently, "It's Dafydd Jones."

"I know your first name." Sherry-Anne lied.

"Well that's good then, I'm not so forgettable," Dafydd stated, and then he said as the waitress put the food in front of them, "Oh good, here's your breakfast and my early lunch."

Sherry-Anne, who had been hungry (until that moment) smelt the food and felt sick; she turned green and ran to the washroom and promptly threw up. When she came out she found Dafydd waiting near at the bathroom door.

He asked, "Are you okay?"

"I'm fine."

Dafydd looked her up and down then he reached out and read her pulse. He looked her up and down noted the growing bulge at her waist line and then deduced, "No, you're not! Are you pregnant? Is it mine?"

"Yes, I'm pregnant and yes, it's your child. I don't sleep around, but it's very complicated," Sherry-Anne stated.

"Why is it complicated? Sherry-Anne that night was magical. I fall hard that night. I love you," Dafydd admitted.

"People don't fall in love in one night," Sherry-Anne replied, sadly.

"I did. Please Sherry-Anne, let me get to know you more and be a part of this child's life," Dafydd begged.

"I told you it's complicated. When I found out I was pregnant and I couldn't find you. I got scared and did something I shouldn't have…"

"Whatever it is we can fix it. I'm here now and I'll help you, sweetheart. Please?" Dafydd begged.

"What are you like my white knight?" Sherry-Anne enquired through tears.

"I want to be. Please, let me help you."

"I …you'll hate me too if I tell you," Sherry-Anne cried.

"Tell me I promise nothing you've done since then will I hold against you," Dafydd promised, "But first come sit down at our table and eat while you tell me."

"Really then you'd be an exception. I did something that was bad," Sherry-Anne confessed.

Dafydd took her arm and guided her to the table where he pulled out the chair for and waited for her to sit down.

"I did something that was criminal," Sherry-Anne continued.

"That doesn't matter to me only you and our baby does. You told me what your aunt and uncle did to you. How they mistreated you and kept your son Caleb from you. I'm sure that had something to do with this. I won't let anything or anyone harm you like that again. I'll hire a good lawyer we will get you out of this. After all you didn't murder anybody did you?" Dafydd asked, "Not that matters. I'm sure you had a good reason and I'll help you hide the body."

"No, I didn't kill anyone, but I drugged someone," Sherry-Anne admitted.

"Okay, so is there any proof?" asked Dafydd trying to cover for her.

"That's all you can think of?" Sherry-Anne enquired surprised, "Not who or why?"

"My first thought was to protect you, but if you want to tell me who and why go ahead, or you can just tell the lawyer if you want," Dafydd offered, crossing his arms and sitting back.

"No, I want to tell you. My high school boyfriend came back. He's my son's father and I was pregnant and I was so scared....,"Sherry-Anne stated as Dafydd started to laugh.

"Why are you laughing? What is so funny?" Sherry-Anne cried outraged.

"I've heard this story before only from the other side," Dafydd answered.

"I don't understand," Sherry-Anne stated puzzled.

"I've met your son's father…"

"You've met Emmett Rogers?" Sherry-Anne cried.

"Yes and I met Lily too. You slept with Emmett?" Dafydd asked.

"I slept with Emmett, slept being the keyword," Sherry-Anne confessed.

"So you drugged him and Lily walked in and she thought you'd slept together willingly?" Dafydd enquired.

"Yes," Sherry-Anne confessed.

"You can fix this Sherry-Anne. Emmett's a reasonable guy. I think he'll be mad, but let this go if only for Caleb's sake. That is if you tell him yourself. You don't love him still?" Dafydd asked.

"I don't know I thought I did but...,"Sherry-Anne said breaking off and starting to cry.

"Could it have been fear and an old crush raising its ugly head that you mistook for love?" Dafydd asked softly.

"Maybe," Sherry-Anne admitted.

"Do you have feelings for me?"

"Yes, I think I do. There's something about you that just makes me feel safe and at home."

"Let's go put it right .Where would Emmett be now?" Dafydd enquired.

"I don't know the police station? Do you really just accept this and me?" Sherry-Anne said shocked that Dafydd cares so much.

"Sherry-Anne, I love you for you. You might not remember; but we talked that night and I told you all my dreams and you told me all yours. It was fate that brought you to me and fate that brought you back. I'm never letting you go sweetie, unless you decide you don't want me," Dafydd admitted.

"If I accept your help can we take it slow?" Sherry-Anne asked, "I don't want to hurt you."

"As slow as you want."

"I'll have nowhere to live I have to find a place," Sherry-Anne confessed.

"I have a huge house and I'd love to have you move in with your son no strings attached," Dafydd insisted.

"I don't know. We'd be in the same house…,"Sherry-Anne protested weakly.

"Sherry-Anne I have four bedrooms. I promised I won't push you and I won't. In fact I'll sign over full custody of our child to you; but I want generous visitation should you decide to leave," Dafydd exclaimed.

"Did anyone tell you you're too good to be true?"

"Wait it gets better .Wait until you hear what I am a doctor of. I'm a coroner," Dafydd stated.

Sherry-Anne started laughing.

"Hey, what's so funny?"

"Is your lab, Davy Jones locker?" Sherry-Anne chortled.

"Like I haven't heard that one before! Now eat your breakfast and then will go fix this problem."

"You really think we can?"

"Yes, I'll get you out of this," Dafydd insisted.

Sherry-Anne wanted to believe that he could help her and she nodded. They ate breakfast and then Dafydd drove her to the hospital to get her car and then drive to the police station to speak with Emmett.

Chapter 20 – Katha and Terrence Investigate

"Your cousin Barney couldn't have been any nicer," Katha commented.

"I just have to see that we don't lose the boy he's job. He'll soon be able to trade in that uniform for an articling job with my old pal Yarby Roland but until then he needs this job," Terrence stated "So I'll watch at the door for other people coming."

"Okay, you do that dear while I try to trigger this drawer," Katha stated moving over to Harold's desk.

"I hear voices Katha. You better hurry up. We can't be caught here." Terrence cried, "Oops false alarm."

"Don't scare me like that Terrence. I've almost got it and there the secret drawer is open."

Katha then extracted a small notebook from the drawer. Katha opened it quickly flipping the pages looking for dates. She reached October and stopped to scan all the entries. Dumbfounded she flipped the pages again, gasping at every turn.

"What is it Katha? Tell me what you've found," Terrence begged.

"You won't believe this I can hardly believe this myself. But I think...,"Katha began when Terrence interrupted saying, "Put the book back Emmett and Kendall are coming down the hall. We have to sneak out into that other office before they see us."

"Terrence what if Emmett could find this book I think it might direct him to the murderer," Katha stated.

"We can't jeopardize Barney's job .Can we go out and pretend we came here looking for Emmett to tell him about the notebook?" Terrence begged.

"That could work! Come on quickly; let's leave before they find us here," Katha exclaimed pulling Terrence through the door and into the outer office beside Harold's office just in time.

"I don't know what you are looking for Emmett. The CSI's went through this office with a fine tooth comb," Kendall complained.

"There has to be something to prove what Brandy said about her," Emmett stated.

Katha and Terrence wait five minutes and then they knocked on the door of Harold's office.

"Who in the hell could that be?" Kendall wondered aloud.

Emmett answered the door to Katha and Terrence and blurted, "Is it the kids? Is something wrong?"

"No, why would you think that there safe on their ski trip," Katha asked then seeing Emmett's face she continued, "They're not on the ski trip? Oh no what's happened to them?"

"Don't jump to conclusions Katha. Let the boy talk," Terrence admonished.

"I phoned the school, they weren't there for attendance. I suspect they are investigating again. Since I couldn't get away I sent my friend Patrolman Alan Barnes to see if they were at the accident site. That was probably an hour ago. Alan had a call to answer first; but he should be there anytime now. As soon as Alan finds them he'll give me a call."

"Emmett do you know about Harold's secret drawer?" blurted Katha.

"A secret drawer? Where is this drawer now how to access it?" Emmett enquired.

"The drawer is right here," Katha explained, showing him how to open the drawer, "I saw Harold open it like this but he didn't see me so I went back out and shut the door."

Emmett flipped open notebook and found the same name Katha found along with notes about her. Emmett is now beginning to believe Brandy had steered them correctly, the woman she believed was the murderer probably was.

"It looks like he may have been blackmailing a lot of people. I can pinpoint them all with the evidence in this book. However Kendall, Brandy was telling the truth. Brandy did know Harold very well have to go to her office and check that out. We need a warrant but, what judge will sign off so quickly?"

"Allow me, I'll call my old friend Robert Eaton," Terrence offered.

"Hello Robert. This is Terrence O'Malley here," Terrence said into his cell phone and then to Emmett he said, "Excuse me for a second while I speak to my old friend Judge Eaton."

Terrence then stepped out in the hall. A few minutes later Terrence comes back in and stated, "Here he faxed it. This is your warrant to search that office. Make it count Emmett nail her to the wall."

"That's kind of the cart before the horse. One word from them, Terrence and Katha and the warrant will be thrown out," Kendall exclaimed.

"I don't know what our talking about. We never saw you go into the office until you received the warrant," Katha replied, "Right Terrence?"

"That's correct. Now go use your warrant, Emmett."

"Thank-you, Terrence. Come on Kendall we have to search an office," Emmett replied.

A few seconds later Sherry-Anne appeared in the hallway with Dafydd following her.

"Is Emmett there? Jenni told me Emmett was here!" Sherry-Anne asked looking around for him.

"No, he's not," Katha lied in a cold voice.

"I need to talk to him. I need to apologise for something. Please do you know where he is?" Sherry-Anne begged.

"What do you need to apologise for? Does it have something to do with him?" Katha shrewdly asked.

"Frankly it's none of your business, Katha."

"That's Mrs. Stewart to you."

"He's down the hall, but he's serving a search warrant; so you'd better wait, missy," Terrence answered.

Katha frowned at him.

"Thank-you," Dafydd mouthed to Terrence.

"Terrence and I are leaving now. Maybe the children are at home. Call us if you hear anything Emmett," Katha shouted into the room.

Sherry-Anne ran down the hall catching Emmett just before he got to the office where he served the warrant to the dead mayor's secretary.

"Emmett I need to talk to you," Sherry-Anne said.

"In case you didn't notice Sherry-Anne the world does revolve around you. I'm trying to do my job here," Emmett stated.

"I know and I wouldn't interrupt if it wasn't important," Sherry-Anne insisted.

"Fine! Kendall can I have five minutes and then will serve the search warrant?" Emmett said visibly upset at the interruption.

"Sure partner, but hurry times a ticking on a murderer."

Emmett took Sherry-Anne to a room nearby where Kendall can't hear. Dafydd follows and listens unseen at the door jam.

"So what's up Sherry-Anne?" Emmett asked.

"I did something wrong for what I thought were all the wrong reasons but I'm sorry for treating you this way," Sherry-Anne rattled off incoherently.

"What are you talking about Sherry-Anne?" Emmett enquired.

"You know I'm pregnant?

"Yes, of course Sherry-Anne. I'm not stupid."

"I'm about four months pregnant. I took one of those tests the earliest ones you could and I knew when you came back that I was pregnant with someone else's baby."

"What?"

"I was scared when I found myself pregnant and then you appeared like a dream from the past," babbled Sherry-Anne.

"Quit babbling and make some sense Sherry-Anne."

"I thought we could start over raise this baby, but Lily was in the way so I slipped something in your drink hoping you think you fathered my baby. I'm ashamed of myself…that I could stoop so low and then when Lily found us together and you were suffering I said nothing. I'm a bitch, a horrible bitch that has ruined your life to save mine. I'm going to tell Lily what I did," Sherry-Anne stopped here.

Emmett looked stunned. He had suspected this but when it was put into words it ripped at his insides.

Dafydd wanted to put his arm around Sherry-Anne but he stayed put listening at the door as Sherry- Anne continued, "I understand you hate me you can't even speak to me. I'll move myself and Caleb out by night fall. You can see your son anytime you want. I know he loves you and you love him." then she continued trying to gauge Emmett's reaction.

Sherry-Anne then started to sob.

"No you don't get to do that Sherry-Anne. Don't you dare cry!! What you did was despicable and downright criminal. I trusted you." Emmett then looked Sherry-Anne straight in the eyes, "I was kind to you. I let you move in with me and I welcomed our son with open arms. I didn't demand a DNA test or yell at you for keeping him from me for seventeen years and then you did this? You ruined my life, you evil bitch!!I had proposed to Lily on Christmas and she was coming to say yes when she saw you. I don't know if she'll ever trust me again. I'm should lay charges against you. It would serve you right to spend time in jail. What kind of person have you turned into?"

"I'm sorry. I'm really sorry Emmett."

"Sorry can't make up for what you did. You're not the girl I fell for in high school. Maybe you should try to find her, before this baby is born and you become its mother," Emmett stated.

"I know you're right. I'm an awful bitch. What kind of person does this? I've wanted to take it back a thousand times, but it can't be taken back. I can only tell you what I did and try to rectify what I did," Sherry-Anne cried regretfully owning up to her deed.

"I know you're sorry I can see that but it doesn't change the fact that you betrayed my trust and took advantage of me for your own gain and the person most hurt is Lily," Emmett stated, sadly.

"Emmett, I'm sorrier than I can say. I'll leave as soon as I'm done here and go to your place and pack," Sherry-Anne answered.

"Do you and Caleb have somewhere to go? Despite everything and for Caleb's sake I could give you some back child support," Emmett offered generously.

"No, I have a place to stay. The baby's father has said we can stay with him. No strings attached," Sherry-Anne answered.

"Is her what triggered your apology you have someone else on the string so you don't need poor deluded Emmett?" Emmett shouted angrily.

"That's enough Rogers," Dafydd stated.

"You! What are you doing here?" Emmett asked suspiciously.

"So Sherry-Anne could tell you what she did without any assistance from me," Dafydd answered.

"Then if that's the case I ask again, what the hell are you doing here?"

"I'm here for her support. Sherry-Anne's pregnant. Can't you be nicer?" Dafydd stated.

"Did she drug you and attempt to pass off her baby as yours?"

"She's apologising. Doesn't that mean anything? Then turning to Sherry-Anne he asked, "Sherry-Anne give us a minute will you?"

"Okay but no more fighting this is my fault, not Dafydd's, Emmett," Sherry-Anne stated as she stepped a small distance away.

"You're the father? I should have known. How you keep twisting yourself into my orbit I don't know," Emmett barked.

"Emmett, may I call you that? I didn't know any of this until today. I met Sherry-Anne in early December at a Christmas party. I fell in love that night. She was pregnant and alone again. So she got scared and did something really stupid but you have to remember what her aunt and uncle did to her. Her head was messed up. She's getting counselling for that and she did come forward of her own accord. I know she's done something awful but if you ever cared for her then you have to try to forgive her."

"Don't you give me the oh so holier than though speech. I've been there for Sherry-Anne. Where have you been?"

"I didn't know where she was. Admittedly we were drunk the night we met and neither of us remembered phone numbers or addresses. But I do love her Emmett I promise you and I'm sorry either of us came between you and Lily. If it's any consolation Lily only dated me once before she told me that she still loved you and Sherry-Anne she loved you, once remember that!!All Sherry-Anne's feelings were all messed up with the past. She was misguided, but scared. As I said she didn't remember my name or know where I was. And then the man who she had thought about for years, dreamed would come save her, did. She couldn't bear to lose you when she was facing a pregnancy without anyone to help her this time," Dafydd cried defending Sherry-Anne.

"You love her. You really love Sherry-Anne?" Emmett asked shocked and surprised all at once.

"Yes, I do!"

"You'll be good to her and Caleb?" Emmett asked making a decision.

"I will. I won't pressure her but I'm hoping she fall in love with me," Dafydd stated.

"Good luck. I hope she doesn't break your heart. And you better not keep my son from me." Emmett said sighing, "You're welcome to her. I have to get back to work."

Then turning to Sherry-Anne he said, "I may forgive you in time but for now I'm still really angry."

Emmett then left and went back to the office to search with Kendall.

Sherry-Anne and Dafydd

"That went well."

"Did it? He hates me."

"He's mad, but he doesn't hate you. At least he's not mad enough to send you to jail. Come on honey let's go to his house and get yours and Caleb's things," Dafydd stated looking back at Emmett.

"Fine let's go," Sherry-Anne answered going down the hall.

"But I have another stop to make at Lily's."

"You're going to tell her what you did?" Dafydd guessed.

"I have to make this right besides what kind of example am I setting for my children if I don't own up to my mistakes."

"I'm proud of you Sherry-Anne."

"Then you'd be the only one," Sherry-Anne stated.

Kendall and Emmett

Kendall took one look at Emmett's face and said, "What did that woman do now?"

"What I expected."

"She did she really drugged you? I'll throttle her."

"Don't do that she's pregnant and then I'd have to arrest you."

"You don't believe that kid's yours do you? The woman lies as easily as she breathes."

"No it's not mine. It's the coroner's."

"How the hell did she get to know him so quickly?"

"It appears she met him in early December."

"Long enough to get pregnant," Kendall stated under her breath and then said, "I'm still going to arrest her."

"Let me handle this Kendall. My boy is going to be hurt."

"Fine but don't let her off the hook."

"I won't she can't be allowed to behave like this."

"Let's get back to work we have to finish searching," Kendall replied.

Emmett and Kendall then searched the office for evidence that would further connect the murderer to Harold's murder. Sherry-Anne made her way to Lily's.

~*0*~

Chapter 21 - She's got my kid

City Hall

"Have you found anything Emmett?" Kendall asked.

"Not a damn thing, yet; it's all in code. This woman is good at hiding that she is a murderer," Emmett said reading the diary.

"Do you want to talk about what Sherry-Anne wanted?"

"No," Emmett said angrily.

"Don't snap at me I'm not Sherry-Anne."

"Sorry partner. I don't want to talk about it."

"She's a bitch anyway. I could guess what she would say."

Emmett allowed himself a brief smirk. Emmett then looked at the warrant.

"Terrence you are at a brilliant man."
Emmett exclaimed.

"What? What did I miss?"

"Terrence got us a warrant for her office and her house, as well as for Harold's office," Emmett exclaimed.

"Good let's take a trip over there," Kendall stated.

"First I have to make a quick call. I don't understand why Alan has called me back. It's been about six hours. Maybe the kids are at home?" Emmett cried, puzzled.

"That's probably it. Call Alan now. I'm sure he just got busy with all that snow outside and hasn't been able to call," Kendall reassured.

Emmett took out his phone and called. No one answered the phone. He called again.

"Alan, answer the phone. Come on answer the phone damn it," Emmett pleaded as he heard a voice; finally he breathed a sigh of relief.

"Alan," Emmett cried.

"Emmett, I was just going to call you," Alan said his voice sounding sad, "I got busy with some calls out in the snow."

"What's wrong Alan?" Emmett asked hearing it in his voice.

"Emmett, she was here at the accident site. I'm so sorry I should have gone out there right away if I had...,"Alan exclaimed as Emmett interrupted with,

"Who? Alan who was there and what happened to Caleb and the girls?" Emmett asked.

"She killed Harold .Emmett and she's got the Banks' girl, Carol and Lily's daughter, Rose," Alan stated.

"Who has them Alan? What about my son Caleb?" Emmett said his voice a little shrill.

"Emmett, I'm so sorry," Alan repeated.

"Quit repeating you and quit being incoherent. Pull yourself together and tell me," Emmett pleaded.

"I don't know who she was. That's all Caleb muttered along with she's got the girls and she's the murderer of parents," Alan explained.

"He's talking about Barbara Franks. I know he is. What has she done to my boy?" Emmett exclaimed.

"Barbara Franks? But she's the *Assistant Crown Attorney*! Is that the she you wouldn't name?" Kendall exclaimed, in the background but Emmett waved her away.

"Barbara Franks stuffed Caleb into his car trunk. He was in the trunk for six hours. The trunk had deteriorated it was quite rusty lucky for Caleb. The trunk had holes in it that he was able to expand on and get out of the trunk," Alan tried to explain over the phone.

"What hospital did they take him to for the hypothermia?" Emmett asked grasping what Alan was saying.

"Happy Valley General," Alan stated.

"Emmett do you want me to drive you?" Kendall asked, after listening into the conversation.

"No can you stay on the warrant and get some evidence on her? She's not getting away with this, but we also have to figure out where she took Carol and Rose."

"Just find my cousin safe and call me when you know how Caleb is and if you find my cousin Carol."

"I'll call you, but try to find the where she took the girls. Any information would be help in this instance. We're flying blind here and those kids lives are at stake."

Emmett rushed into the hall where he ran right into Terrence and Katha.

"What is wrong, Emmett?" Terrence cried.

"I have to go. Barbara has hurt Caleb."

"What? How?" Terrence asked.

"She put him in a trunk. He has hypothermia and they're taking him to hospital."

"But you said the girls were with Caleb. Where are Rose and Carol?" Katha demanded.

"Barbara subdued Caleb. I assume he subdued then too and then she took them. What am I going to do? I can't be in two places at once and how can I tell Lily that someone has taken the girls again?" Emmett stated.

"Barbara Franks has Carol and Rose? How did this happen? Oh my God, Terrence this can't be occurring again," Katha cried and then as the realization set in she babbled hysterically, "My girls, my babies. She's got my babies. Do something, Terrence."

"Emmett, you can't do anything for your boy right now; but you could save the girls," Terrence begged.

"We can't ask him to do that," Katha exclaimed, "Kendall can find her cousin, Carol and my Rose. Can't you, Kendall?"

"I'll go to Caleb, Emmett. Go be with your son," Katha insisted.

"I'm so torn. I know that Caleb would want me to find them, but someone has to be with Caleb. He's been hurt and someone needs to take his statement. Maybe he can point us in the right direction. I'll have to call Lily and Sherry-Anne so they can to go to Caleb, too," Emmett said.

"We'll go to Caleb and stay with him Emmett. You just find Carol and Rose, and bring my girls home safely to us. If he says anything that will help you find the girls we'll call you," Katha exclaimed a tear slipping out of her eye.

"It's okay Katha. Emmett will find them for us." Terrence stated reassuring Katha and putting his arm around her.

"Sherry-Anne it is Emmett," Emmett said into the phone.

"Oh hello, I'm here with Lily. I've told her everything. She's really mad, but you're a lucky man she's a wonderful woman. You might just get her back someday," Sherry-Anne says flippantly into her cell phone.

"Sherry-Anne something has happened to Caleb…,"Emmett began,

"What happened to Caleb was he in an accident? Is he okay?" Sherry-Anne asked.

"Sherry-Anne he's on his way to hospital. He has hypothermia. The thing is I can't be at the hospital...." Emmett tried to explain as Sherry-Anne interrupted; "Your job always comes first. What about our child? If he has hypothermia that's serious Emmett .He needs you."

"I want to be there Sherry-Anne. You know I love Caleb but Rose and Carol have been taken by the same maniac that harmed our son. Caleb would want me to save them," Emmett stated.

"Someone took Rose and Carol?" Sherry-Anne blurted, as Lily hearing this gasped and demanded, "Give me your phone Sherry-Anne."

Sherry-Anne handed her cell phone to Lily.

"Emmett this is Lily. What did you just tell Sherry-Anne about Rose and Carol?" Lily exclaimed.

"The kids were onto something .Apparently they skipped school and went to search the accident site for the container the squares were in trying to connect it to the murderess. The problem was that she was looking for it too. Lily there is no way to sugar coat this I believe the murder is Barbara Franks. Barbara has taken Rose and Carol," Emmett explained.

"Barbara is the murderer? But that makes no sense. Barbara would hurt anyone. She likes Rose. She's known Rose since she was nine years old. She wouldn't harm her. She just wouldn't!!" protested Lily.

"Barbara was having an affair with Harold, and then she blackmailed him, but he was ready to turn her in so she killed him at least that's what we believe," Emmett explained.

"Barbara would do that. You have to be mistaken," Lily continued to protest with disbelief.

"I have to tell you, it is possible. Brandy Calders has confirmed Barbara had an affair with Harold," Emmett stated.

"Brandy Calders of the police force? But how would she know?" Lily protested.

"Brandy has Harold's child, a little girl Hannah Robin who was born October 31st last year." Emmett explained, "And my son, Caleb is in the hospital. She locked him in his car trunk."

"Caleb was harmed? Is he going to be okay?" Lily asked.

"I don't know but I know that Caleb would want me to rescue the girls and I can't be in two places at once. I have to go now. I have to see if she has the girls at her house."

"Please find them Emmett. Try not to worry about Caleb. Sherry-Anne and I will head to the hospital to be with Caleb and we'll keep you updated." Lily stated, "Go now. Find my daughter and Carol."

"I can't tell you how much this means to me," Sherry-Anne says as Lily hands her the phone.

"Don't be too grateful Sherry-Anne. I'm doing this for Emmett and Caleb not you. I'm sorry your son is hurt and I'm truly sorry for the pain that causes you. I think Caleb is fine young man despite his mother .He must get that from his father," Lily cried, coldly.

"I don't blame you for talking to me like that. I deserved it. I'm just glad you're a big enough person to not take out your anger on my son. I know that Caleb respects and cares about you. Thank-you, for that Lily! I know it could have been easy to welcome my son when I appeared so suddenly," Sherry-Anne exclaimed.

Lily couldn't believe what she was hearing. Sherry-Anne was in crisis yet she was nice to Lily. Had Lily misjudged her? No Sherry-Anne had drugged Emmett and she should pay for that.

"Dafydd Jones is waiting outside for me I'm sure he'd give us both a ride to the hospital," Sherry-Anne continued.

"Dafydd? You know Dafydd?" Lily cried.

"He's the father of my baby," Sherry-Anne admitted.

Of course he was, Lily thought you bitch you just want to ruin my life. I hate you!! She tried not to show this to Sherry-Anne but the words came out bitterly, "Well isn't that cozy? You have had both the men in my life."

"If it's any consolation they were mine first," Sherry-Anne stated wickedly.

"I'll accept the ride since it is Dafydd's car; but I really don't want to have anything more to do with you, Sherry-Anne. I would be most happy to never see you again, but I know that's impossible since I care about Caleb and Emmett. So I will call a truce for now. But I'll be watching you. Remember however I'm doing this for Caleb and Emmett not you."

"I hope that in time you will be able to forgive me," Sherry-Anne stated regretfully.

"Let's just go for the truce for now and go from there."

Lily and Sherry-Anne put on their coats and boots and went out to Dafydd's car.

"Is everything okay?" Dafydd asked puzzled.

"No Caleb..," Sherry-Anne exclaimed before dissolving into tears.

"Caleb has been hurt by a mad woman who has taken my daughter and my cousin," Lily explained.

"Oh no, I'm so sorry. Let me take you to Caleb. I take it you're going too Lily?" Dafydd asked.

"I'm going for Emmett and Caleb and my daughter."

"It will be okay Sherry-Anne. We'll be at the hospital soon," Dafydd soothed.

"So you two are together now?" Lily asked.

"That is up to Sherry-Anne she knows where I stand," Dafydd stated.

"I hope you know what you're getting into Dafydd," Lily stated.

Sherry-Anne glared at Lily.

"I'm going in with eyes wide open. I also know that under that hard exterior that Sherry-Anne has perfected, lays a heart that is sweet caring loving and exactly the woman I've always wanted," Dafydd says smiling at Sherry-Anne in his car mirror.

Sherry-Anne smiled back at Dafydd and for a moment Lily saw what Emmett and Dafydd saw in Sherry-Anne and it scared her she might actual like Sherry-Anne. But then Lily thought Sherry-Anne has many faces should I really trust this one? Lily would wait with Caleb and then cut ties as much as she could with this evil woman. She certainly would never ever trust her again.

~0~

Chapter 22 – The Killer Revealed

Barbara opened the trunk of her car in her garage.

"So what am I going to do with you, girls?"

"You could let us go," Rose exclaimed. "Please Ms. Franks?"

"I can't! You know what she did," Barbara stated.

"Know what who did?" Carol asked confused.

"We don't know what you're talking about," Rose insisted.

"Good try girls. It won't work."
Barbara announced, "Now come
along into the house and down into
the basement."

Rose and Carol went ahead of
Barbara as she held the gun behind
them and down the stairs into the
basement. Rose snuck a look back at
Barbara; somehow Barbara seemed so
different from the Barbara in mom's
office and it wasn't just the gun.
Something about the way Barbara
held herself erect was totally
different. Her hair was combed a
different way too. Rose stifled a laugh
at that thought that she was in danger
and all she had noticed was a change
in a murderer's hair. How silly! Rose
should be thinking about how to get
away.

"You can sit on the sofa for now."

"You could let us go. You've known me for six years doesn't that count Ms. Franks?" Rose argued.

"It should count, but then I'm not Barbara," she said bluntly.

"I don't understand," Rose exclaimed.

"All you need to know is that Barbara really doesn't want me to kill you .She's fighting me so you live for now."

"You're not Barbara?" Carol asked, confused.

"Do I look like a Barbie doll?"

"No, of course you don't look like a Barbie doll," Rose answered seizing the chance to mollify their kidnapper.

"I always thought you were smart, Rose Brooksfield. Despite your biological parents you seem to emulate Lily. I admire that woman she's so put together and sure of herself. Barbara admires her but doesn't like her; but that's only because she wants her job."

"What should we call you then?" Carol asked.

"The name's Ann. I named myself when we were young. I'm Barbie's best friend," Ann explained.

"How did you choose your name?" Rose replied.

"I'm one of a kind and the name is special. That's why I took the name; after all I couldn't just be she could I?"

"Are you like Barbara's twin?" Carol asked, not understanding.

"No you silly little twit. Barbara's still in here; she's just not able to come out. She's a bundle of emotions right now none of which she can stand. Such a foolish girl!! She can't stand up for herself let's people walk all over then she retreats into silence so I have to handle all her messes."

"Oh, are there anymore of you?" Rose asked boldly.

"There's Holly but she hasn't come out in awhile. She's too playful and if you think Barbara's bad you should meet Holly. She plays it all sweet and innocent gets the guy hot and bothered and then retreats to have someone else take over when it gets to the hard stuff."

"No Ken or some other man?" Carol suppressed a laugh.

"Is everything a joke to you Carol? I must have misjudged you I thought you were a lot nicer."

"Carol making fun of her is very rude," admonished Rose.

"I'm sorry," Carol immediately stated.

"You should listen to your friend Carol. Rose has manners you'd be wise to emulate. I'll excuse you this time, but only because you are grieving your parents and you apologized so quickly. Did you get the concert tickets I sent you?"

"I don't understand what you're talking about what concert tickets?" Carol enquired.

"The Disaster Brewing concert .I sent you the tickets in the mail and of course all those other prizes you 'won.' You won't be able to go to see Disaster Brewing now, though."

"You killed my parents and my grandfather and you send me concert tickets and other prizes?"

"I felt bad that you'd lost your parents." Ann explained, "I thought I do something nice for you to cheer you up. You've spoiled that all now."

"That was so nice of you. We are sorry for spoiling it," Rose says mollifying once again trying to keep Ann liking them.

"You are a sweet girl, Rose."

"Why are you being nice to this whack job?" Carol whispered through clenched teeth.

"Do you really think I can't hear your pathetic whispering Carol? I am not a whack job. I guess I was totally wrong you're simply don't know how to be a nice girl at all."

Ann then turned to one side as if conducting a conversation with someone, "No, Barbara. What am I supposed to do? Yes, I thought of that? You were the one that locked Caleb in the trunk. What do you mean that wasn't you? Who else is there? Who is Terri?"

Rose thought about charging past her but Ann still held the gun and was waving it around while she talked.

"Is everything okay? Is there something we can do to help you?" Rose asked.

"It seems that Terri came out to play. I've never met her, but Barbara says she's one of us."

"Can I talk to Terri?" Rose enquired.

"No, Barbara says Terri is a predator. She hates young girls and she also flirts outrageous with young teen men. "

"If she likes teen men then why did she lock Caleb in that trunk in the snow so he could die?"

"There's more of a chance then I would have given him. I hate men. They should all die and make the world better," Ann stated.

"Do you hate us too?" Rose asked, worried.

"Do I hate you? No, I'm indifferent to you both. I only worry about one person besides myself and that's Barbara. I keep Barbara from all harm."

"We would never hurt Barbara. I've known her a long time ever since I was nine years old and Carol met her when she was eleven. We like her. Right, Carol?"

Carol just nodded her head.

"You know what Barbara did so how could you like any of us?" Ann protested.

"So maybe they deserved it. Right, Carol?" Rose stated.

"Maybe my grandfather did. He wasn't a nice man; but my mom and dad didn't," Carol replied.

"Sweetie I hate to tell you this but your Dad slept with Barbara. He slept with a lot of women he was a hound dog. Gerald said he'd leave his wife for Barbara but he made the mistake of introducing his father-in law to her; instead of keeping her by his side he put Barbara in your grandfather's path. He laughed and used her like collateral with his father-in law," Ann said.

"Ann I don't think you should be telling Carol this. Girls love their fathers and they don't want them to have done any wrong. It hurts their self-image, I should know when all those stories came out about my dad it nearly killed me," Rose rebuked gently.

"Girls love their fathers? I guess you're correct when it comes to Barbie. Barbara loved our father despite what he did to us. She still doesn't know what he did. I managed to hide that from her. I took her place when he came in our room and crawled in our bed. I hated him and made sure that he couldn't do what he did to us anymore when we got older. The bastard paid us lots of money to stay quiet. As if I'd ever tell anyone. Oops, I told you two but you'll not tell anyone will you especially you Rose because you understand. Don't you?"

"I am so sorry that happened to you. What an evil man unfit to be a father...,"Rose blurted angrily before she was interrupted.

"I knew you'd understand that men are truly evil," Ann replied, "Did your fathers do that, too?"

"My father wouldn't do that," Rose replied.

"Nor mine," Carol answered.

"You were lucky they died before they could show their true colors."

"No father should do that to his child. If people had known he would have been put in jail," Rose stated.

"Oh, the innocence of youth. He was important person. People who are important don't do those things they don't commit crimes. No one believes they could do anything wrong .They must have a rebellious crazy daughter who needs to be quietly committed," Ann replied sadly.

"I am so sorry," Rose said with tears in her eyes.

"You believe me?" Ann cried surprised like no one had ever believed her.

"Of course we do." Carol answered, "Your father was evil."

"Yes he was. "Commented Ann, "I do like you two girls. Barbara isn't always accurate when it comes to people, but it seems she knew you well. She really likes you. She even fought with me when I thought about killing you. Maybe we could keep you here, hidden. I have a wine cellar. Or rather Barbara does."

"Please we will keep your secrets. Like I said no father should do what was done to and the mayor sounds just as bad right Carol?"

"Er...I guess you're right grandpa deserved it," Carol replied.

"Fine, then be good girls and help me move these blow-up beds and sleeping bags in there. Then I'll think about how long to keep you and what to do with you in the meantime," Ann stated, excited pointing to blow up beds in the corner and sleeping bags.

Rose and Carol help her carry the already blown –up mattresses into the wine room along with the sleeping bags. Rose wondered about the fact that Ann had already had blown up mattress; obviously a plan had been in place otherwise why blow the beds? For moment Rose thinks about overcoming her but she notices she's still carrying the gun.

"I have to leave you both in here. The room is sound proof and temperature controlled for Barbara's wines which I have removed. We can't have underage girls drinking. Sit tight I'll bring you some dinner later and some more blankets as I know it's a little cool in here. Maybe I'll even bring you a television and the apple television if you're good," Ann stated locking the door with a key.

"Is she gone?" Carol asked.

"Yes, she's gone," Rose replied.

"I don't understand why she kept saying she was Ann. Is she crazy?" Carol asked terrified.

"It's a mental disorder. I read about this. It's called Dissociative identity disorder," Rose replied smugly.

"Why would you just read about this? Do you know someone who is that sick?" Carol enquired.

"Well when I was home sick from school with my appendicitis surgery, I watched Sybil on one of Grandma Katha's old DVD's. This girl in that movie was named Sybil and she was played by Sally Fields I think something or other; anyway she had this disorder where she acted like several different people because she was abused as a child," Rose exclaimed.

"This is starting to make sense. Ann says Barbara's father abused her," Carol answered.

"Some of them have eating disorders and she sure looks like she does. She looks like a Barbie doll with her skinny waist and her spindly arms. We could probably overcome her if she didn't have that gun," Rose claimed.

"I'm scared Rose. What if this other personality Terri hates us and comes out?"

"That's why we have to be nice until we can escape."

"Good thinking .I'll try to pick the lock but this one is one of those really good locks. The type of lock that is almost impossible to pick," Carol claimed "Do you have booby pin or something to poke it with?"

"No. I didn't wear any bobby pins today, but I have a nail kit. Will that do?"

Rose handed Carol the nail kit. Carol opens it to find a nail clipper a nail file and small nail scissors.

"This will do nicely. I can take apart these scissors. See in two parts," Carol cried taking the scissors apart.

"Are you sure that will work?"

"These can then be used as tools to poke the lock like this. I'm warning you though this could take a long time." Carol answered, "It is one of the best locks on the market."

~0~

Chapter 23 - Who am I?

A few hours later

"Carol, stop whatever it is you're doing and hide the tools. Someone is coming," Rose stated.

After a few seconds Carol too heard the pitter-patter of steps on the stairs. The tread was soft but definitely adult like.

"Did you really think I wouldn't know what you were doing Carol?" the voice said.

"How do you know what I was doing? We're in the basement."

"I have cameras down here in the wine room. See, there. I just don't trust anyone not to steal all my wine that I moved out of here. I remembered your grandfather bragging about how good you were at picking locks like your no good dad,"

"Sorry?" Carol said.

"I'll excuse it for now after all you don't know us well," Ann cried then turned sideways and started whispering to thin air as if she were talking to someone. Then she turned back to them and said, "Hello," as if Ann hadn't already spoken to them.

Rose stared at Ann now wearing along brown wig. She stands defiantly like a teen who is trying to act cool Rose realizes this isn't Ann anymore but perhaps Terri or Holly?

"Hello, is it Holly?" Rose exclaimed hoping she guessed correctly.

"Oh, you know of me? Good. That will save time. I need your advice." Holly stated conspiratorially.

"Our advice what would you need our advice about?"

"There are people at the front door. I've never seen a policeman except in television shows. An Emmett Rogers and Kendall Evans are at our door. Barbara's memories and Ann's says they are police. Barbra also says he's that boy's daddy. I'm scared I don't know what to do. They may want to hurt us, or you and Carol," Holly cried sounding like a very young scared ten year old.

"Emmett is really nice. He won't harm any of you."

"He sounds awful nice, but he's the boy's daddy and we left Caleb to die," Holly cried, "Ann is yelling at me to let her come out; that she can handle this."

"Do you think Ann can handle this?" Rose asked.

"I don't know. She seems awful mad. Ann says Mr. Roger's evil and that he'll harm us. He cheated on your mother, the divine Miss Lily. Is that true?" Holly asked.

"An evil woman drugged Emmett and made it look that way. Really Emmett is sweet and kind. He thinks of others first. That's why he's a policeman. He won't harm any of you. He'll be kind you'll see," Rose explained.

"Oh the poor man, I feel sorry for this Emmett. Did your mother forgive him?" She asked sounding different and standing differently again.

"She doesn't know yet; but I think she'll forgive him when she finds out," Rose stated, "Are you Terri?"

"Yes, of course I am Terri. You are clever you seem to know who each of us are. It must because you are a genuinely nice person, Rose. I'll listen to you; if you think I should. You're sure I should let him in? That he won't treat us unkindly?" Terri asked as the doorbell pealed again.

"He will treat you with all the kindness and respect he can possibly give and help you all. Especially if he sees Carol and I are okay."

"Is that what you think too Carol?" Terri enquired.

"Yes, Mr. Rogers is a good man. You should let him in. He'll help you and he never judges," Carol replied.

"Ann did promise that if Caleb lived we'd take our lumps; so I guess we have to let them in but we are all afraid. What about the others with him and what will happen when Barbara finds out what we've done?"

"She'll forgive you. You were only protecting her," Rose exclaimed.

"Do you hate Ann and Barbie for killing your family members, Carol?" Terri asked.

"No. I loved my parents; but it sounds like you all regret what happened to them. Did Grandpa do something else bad to Barbara?" Carol said wanting to placate her and get her to let Mr. Roger's and the other police in."

"Yes, your grandfather did but we don't want to talk about it."

There was more banging heard at the front door and it sounded like a police ramming tool was being used.

"You should answer the door. If you don't they'll just break in." Rose stated, "Emmett will help you more if you let him in and he doesn't have to break in."

"The door is steel plated it might take him awhile. I don't know if we should wait or let them in. They might not understand about us and how were here to protect Barbara. I think I'm going to have to reveal myself to Barbie and ask Barbara what to do. We've hidden so much from her that I hope she can handle it. Most of all she won't be happy that we took you. I won't tell her about how Ann poisoned the squares but she might find out. She'll hate us for that; she loved Harold even though he harmed her again and again," Terri cried troubled.

Terri seemed to zone out and her eyes glazed over. Then just as suddenly she seemed to be more alert but she looked terrified and she confessed to Carol and Rose, "Barbara says it's time to admit what we did, but that she can't do it. Ann doesn't want to, she says just kill the cops. I'm scared too," Terri answered.

"Can I talk to Ann for a moment?" Rose asked.

"I don't think that's a good idea," Carol exclaimed.

"I know that's a good idea. If she comes out she might stay and hurt the policeman," Terri cried grimacing.

Her face then contorted slightly as she became Ann.

"What do you want Rose? Do you think you can talk me out of this? You can't and now I have to do the dirty work that my sisters are too scared to do."

"What are you going to do?" Rose asked though she knew.

"As if you didn't know I'm going to kill those police people so they'll leave us all alone," Ann stated.

"Was there ever a man who was nice to you just because he was nice?" Asks Rose

"You mean nice to Barbara?" Ann asked puzzled, "More than when I was young our grandfather brought us toys and took us to see a Disney movie and other children's plays. He bought us candy, he told us not to tell our daddy and to eat the candy until after supper. Our grandfather was so kind. We loved him so, but our Daddy stopped him from coming. We couldn't even go to his funeral," Ann answered.

"I'm so sorry that you had such an awful person as your father. Your grandfather sounds lovely," Carol commented.

"He read me stories and tucked me in bed .He took me to see the Nutcracker once," Ann replied sounding like Barbara

"That must have been wonderful," Rose stated keeping Ann thinking about positive memories.

Ann looked troubled and then she looked pained as she declared, "Barbara is yelling. She wants to come out and speak with you."

"I'm sorry girls. I'm sorry for everything. I don't know exactly what has happened but I know it's bad," Barbara cried out in the next breath.

"It will be okay Ms. Franks," Rose comforted.

"Someone is ringing the door .Will you answer it girls? I'm afraid they'll shoot me."

"Of course we will, "Rose and Carol chimed together.

Carol and Rose then ran up the stairs and shouted through the door, "Don't shoot were opening the door. It's Carol Banks, and Rose Brooksfield."

Carol and Rose open the door to Emmett and Kendall and some other police personnel.

"Are you okay? Did she hurt you two? Where's Barbara?" Emmett asked, looking beyond them.

"We're fine," Carol and Rose answered.

"Barbara you're under arrest for four counts of murder, one count of attempted murder and three counts of kidnapping."

"Barbara isn't here. She is scared so we took over," answered the person now in control to Emmett.

"What in the hell are you talking about Barbara?" Kendall shouted.

"Don't shout at her Kendall."

"I don't like her she's mean. I thought you said police were nice, Rose?" Holly responded.

"It will be okay, Holly. Kendall gets a little angry when she's scared too," Rose stated.

"Is this a defense? Or are you really...?" Emmett asked.

"She isn't faking Emmett. She has many different people inside her. I believe she has dissociative disorder, you know multiple personality, "Rose stated.

"So who is this?" Emmett asked.

"I don't know. I just know it isn't Barbara," Rose stated.

"I am Ann Hadley and you are Emmett Rogers," Ann cried taking over.

"I'm Detective Emmett Rogers," Emmett answered.

"Barbara seems to think we can trust you," she replied.

"You aren't Ann," Emmett stated noting the different stance.

"No, I'm Terri. The rest of them are scared so I'm handling this."

"Terri did Barbara put my son in the trunk?" Emmett asked.

"No, that was me .It was the only way I could save him for Ann wanted to kill him then." Terri explained, "Is your boy okay?"

"Caleb is in the hospital I need to go to him but first I have to make sure you are okay," Emmett stated.

"I hope he'll be okay," Terri exclaimed.

"Are you really buying this crap Emmett? This crazy act? She's been found out so she pretends she has multiple personalities just so she can get a cushy room in a mental hospital," Kendall shouted at Emmett then turning to Terri she commented angrily, "It won't wash with me honey."

"I like you Emmett .I don't like her," She responded her voice changing again into a little girl voice.

"Who am I talking to now?" Emmett asked motioning to Kendall to be quiet.

"Holly." she answered, quietly.

"Come on Emmett these are all just made up names. She's faking, don't be fooled," Kendall exclaimed.

"Kendall be quiet I'm listening to Holly," Emmett implored.

"Holly's gone, that scary lady chased her away. I'm Terri. We really are all sorry you know, Ann most of all."

"Why is Ann so sorry?" Emmett asks leading the conversation.

"Barbara says we shouldn't say. Something about incrimination?" Terri stated, "We should only tell Dr. Hayward. She called him once; but Ann wouldn't let her go to get help."

"See what did I tell you Emmett? Dr. Hayward is a doctor on that old soap, *All My Children.* She's making this up as she goes along," Kendall responded.

"Actually Ms. Evans, Dr. Robert Hayward is psychiatrist. He has a practice uptown with Dr. Jeffries at 156 Acorn Street," Carol interrupted.

"Brat," Kendall said under her breath.

"Would you like to see Dr. Hayward? We could get him to come to the station. You know we have to take you there until we can get a judge to agree that you should go to get some help," Emmett agreed.

"We are so tired. Can we sleep there?" Terri asked.

"Of course you can. It must be hard to deal with all of this. There must be reasons behind it that we aren't aware of," Emmett soothed.

"You have no idea. Barbara was so unhappy. And that horrible man wanted to take away her job. She'd already lost so much we couldn't let him humiliate her in more. She'll lose her job now, won't she?" Terri asked.

"You know that Barbara and all of you need some help. Barbara has needed help for a long time and you tried to provide that, but you know that help has gone too far now. She needs professional help," Emmett answered gently.

"We can't keep killing people. I told Ann that we couldn't go on this way after she killed Grace-Ellen Singer with that rat poison. Although she seemed to think it was funny killing a rat with rat poison. She was a terrible woman a worse blackmailer than Harold," Terri stated.

"And Harold? How did you kill him?" Emmett asked.

"I didn't kill him. Ann did. He called Barbara over to his house pretending he loved her that he would leave his wife for her .Ann took over to protect Barbara. He hurt Ann. He degraded her, made fun of her. He ripped her clothes."

"He raped her and then laughed. Barbara came out too soon .She found her clothes ripped and she knew what had happened. She said she go to the police he laughed again and he said he had evidence that she had helped him in a crime and demanded money. Barbara had never committed a crime; but he said she either paid him money or he would make it look like she had. Barbara said she would pay him installments and pretended she still loved him. She brought the orange squares over for him knowing that he was allergic to ginger. She would have left and not give them to him; but Ann was angry and Ann gave them to him. Then Barbara found out they had all died and she knew what had happened .she has been trying to find a way out she almost confessed to you several times but we stopped her. Barbara wants all of this to end. So end it!!"Terri cried.

Suddenly her face contorted and a voice was heard saying from Barbara's lips, "I told you not to tell. We're all doomed."

Then the person in control grabbed Carol and pulling a knife from her pocket she placed it at Carol's throat.

"Who are we talking to now?" Emmett asked softly.

"I'm not telling you my name they don't know about me, but I'm actually the one who killed not Ann," the person answered in husky voice with an English accent.

"And why are you here now?"

"They're too scared to take charge but I'm not. Let us go or I'll kill Carol."

Kendall raised her gun and took aim but Emmett pushed her gun down and stated, "That's not the way to handle this."

"I respect you Emmett Rogers. Man to man you are a nice bloke."

"I'm sure you don't want to have to kill again. Can we end this? Can I talk to Barbara?" Emmett enquired.

"Just a moment, I have to think about this."

The eyes seemed to lose focus and the face contorted and then the person in charge dropped the knife and said, "What is going on? I don't understand this. Why did I have a knife to Carol's throat? I don't harm people."

"It's okay Barbara it's going to be all okay." Emmett said gently, "I have to read your rights to you now but we'll get some help for you. We'll get your doctor to come to the station as soon as possible."

"Read me my rights? What did I do wrong?"

"You have the right to remain silent and refuse to answer questions. Do you understand?"

"Yes, I think so," Barbara answered.

"Anything you do say may be used against you in a court of law. Do you understand?"

"Yes," Barbara answered again.

"You have the right to consult an attorney before speaking to the police and to have an attorney present during questioning now or in the future. Do you understand?"

"Yes but my head hurts so," Barbara complained.

"If you cannot afford an attorney, one will be appointed for you before any questioning if you wish. Do you understand?"

Barbara said nothing, but Emmett continued,

"If you decide to answer questions now without an attorney present you will still have the right to stop answering at any time until you talk to an attorney. Do you understand? Knowing and understanding your rights as I have explained them to you, are you willing to answer my questions without an attorney present?"

"She's not here anymore but I am, I'm Ann and I understand," Ann cried.

Emmett put handcuffs on her and secures them behind her back.

"I'm sorry Rose; but I'm especially sorry for hurting you Carol. I didn't think about how it would hurt anyone else. I'm so sorry for taking your parents from you," Ann stated.

"It's time to go and let Carol heal," Kendall declared.

Kendall then turned to Rose and Carol.

"I called your mom Rose should be here soon and mom is coming for you, Carol," Kendall stated.

"I'll take her in Emmett you go to Caleb," Kendall exclaimed as Ann visibly cringed.

"No, I made a promise to Barbara and I'm keeping it." Emmett insisted, "You can take her to the car only and be gentle."

"Fine, but I still think she's faking," Kendall claimed.

"You can think what you like Kendall, but I believe her," Emmett admitted, smiling gently at Ann.

Kendall lead her to the car and said, "I'm going with you of course number one I'm your partner and two I'm your back-up. Here's Lily and Amelia. We'll be waiting in the car but hurry up."

"Rose? Carol? Are you two all right I've been worried out of my mind," Lily cried coming upon the scene, followed by Amelia who just threw her arms around Carol.

"It's okay Amelia see we're okay," Carol said surprised, by how much Amelia is showing she cares about her.

"I couldn't bear to lose you. I can't lose anyone else," Amelia stated.

Lily started crying too.

"It's okay Lily. "Emmett stated taking Lily in his arms.

"How is Caleb .You two were at the hospital weren't you?" Emmett asked.

"The doctor says he'll be fine. They're going to keep him for few days. He said for you to save Rose and Carol, but be gentle with Barbara. He said something strange he says she isn't Barbara. That she has different personalities," Lily relayed, "Katha is staying with him and watching over him, with Sherry-Anne. So don't worry he isn't alone."

"Thank God. That kid is a chip off the old block. He knew, somehow he knew that Barbara has dissociative disorder," Emmett said letting go of Lily, "I have to go now .Get the girls checked over."

"But we're fine," insisted Carol and Rose.

"It is procedure, so you have to follow it!" Emmett said to the girls then turning to Lily he said, "Thanks for being so kind to Sherry-Anne after what she did."

"I will take them to be checked out Emmett and we will stay there until you get there to be with Caleb," Lily stated.

"Thanks Lily."

Emmett then left.

"So you're back together?" Rose asked.

"Not really."

"Mom is there any chance you and Emmett would date again?" Rose asked.

"I don't know. If we did we would have to take it slow," Lily replied.

"I can understand that. Just so you know Caleb and I really aren't dating. We're good friends and we've seen how much your both hurting. Emmett loves you Mom. Don't throw that away because I know you love him too," Rose stated as Amelia and Carol nod in agreement.

"I'll think about it. How did you get to be so smart?" Lily asked.

"I'm growing up but I'm always going to be your little girl, never forget that Mom." Rose insisted, "When I thought one of Barbara's alters would kill us all I could think was I wanted my mother."

"I'm sorry baby. I'm sorry we didn't figure this out sooner. It seems like I'm not keeping you safe that you're facing too much. Is it my fault? Maybe there is a curse?"

"No mom just a few crazy people out there that unfortunately are gravitating towards us," Rose answered.

"You always tell me that curse nonsense is just that nonsense, so drop this kind of talk Lily and just be glad you and Carol are safe. Now let's go," Amelia exclaimed.

Carol and Amelia climbed into the back seat of the car and Lily and Rose into the front as they drive through the heavy snow and to the hospital.

~0~

Chapter 24 – Epilogue

A week later

Lily was glad that Carol's situation had
been settled. Amelia had wanted to adopt
her but the court thought a two parent family
with the police chief and his wife would be
best. Carol seemed happy with them and it
wasn't like she didn't visit Rose as much as
she did before. Regan was mothering her so
Carol had a stable home. Regan also had
gotten Carol to admit she needed some help
dealing with the grief so that had made
Carol less angry.

Sherry-Anne had admitted before the court
her crime and was now serving 500 hours of
community service for drugging Emmett. It
was a little sentence given the gravity of the
crime, but Lily and Caleb had gone to bat
for her just so Caleb wouldn't lose his
mother.

All seemed right with the world and as Lily looked around she saw family not of blood but of bonds that were forged from love.

There was a big turnout for this baby shower and lots of love. She had planned on a one person shower just for Suzy; but Suzy fell sorry for Brandy that she had so little for Brandy's baby, Harriet Robin.

The games had played the prizes had been won including the overnight trip to Niagara Falls. The slab cake with a white frosty half chocolate and half white had been well received.

"This has been a great shower," Katha answered.

"Look even the guys look happy," Lily stated.

"You hand a guy some food and a beer and they are always happy. It's good that her colleagues from the police department could come and a lot of them brought triple gifts one for each baby," Katha exclaimed.

"Look how happy Suzy looks," Lily smiled.

"It's probably the first time she hasn't had her arms full of babies. Look at Caleb and Emmett cooing over them," Katha says "Those little baby girls Emma and Abigail are really happy with them."

"Emmett is wonderful with children," Lily stated.

"He'll make a fine father someday," Katha stated as Lily blushes thinking of that.

"This was a great idea to include Brandy as the recipient of the shower and inviting all the men to the shower," Katha said approvingly.

Lily looked at the gifts in the corner all unwrapped and on display for both women's babies. Car seats for all of them and lots of clothing. Lily had never seen so many small pieces of clothing.

"Brandy has Harold's child, which makes Harriet Robin, Carol's aunt, therefore she's family," Lily exclaimed.

"That's true isn't it? Look at that Carol is holding Harriet Robin and she looks happy. The first time I've see her smile since…,"Katha cried, surprised.

"I am so glad .Maybe things will get better for Carol now. I'm also glad that Caleb has recovered."

"Me too. All our children are fine," Katha stated.

"So you've adopted Caleb?"

"Of course I have. His father is important to you and then that little rascal took my heart," Katha answered.

"Your heart is so big Grandma Katha. He's a lucky kid to have you in his corner."

"Look at that baby laugh at Carol. I believe she's actually listening to Carol," Katha stated making small talk.

Carol enjoyed holding Harriet Robin. Carol looked at the little baby that is her Aunt, funny that a baby could be her Aunt. She couldn't believe this was her aunt. So strange that she was fifteen almost sixteen years older than her aunt. The little girl was family though. Poor baby she'd lost her father, too. Not that grandfather would have been a good father he wasn't to mommy.

"Her name is Harriet Robin, Carol but I call her Robin," Brandy cried handing Carol a bottle.

"Did you know that Robin was one of my middle names?"

"Your mother told me that it was when I begged her to give me a family name."

"You spoke with my mother? She knew about Harriet Robin?"

"She gave me some presents for her sister when Robin was born."

"She looks like a Robin especially when she's hungry," Carol giggled.

If you want to watch Robin for bit I'll get something to eat."

"Sure I can do that maybe I'll even babysit my aunt from time to time," Carol stated.

"I'm sure she'd like that I know would."

Brandy then walked over to the food table for another piece of fruit since she said cake wasn't on her diet.

Poor little baby. Carol thought. The baby's name, Robin reminded her though of something her mother had said to her when she was younger. Carol decided to recite this rhyme to Harriet Robin

"Cold and raw the north wind doth blow

Bleak in the morning early,

All the hills are covered with snow,

And winters now come fairly.

Wind doth blow and we shall have snow,

And what will poor robin do then, poor thing?

He'll sit in a barn and keep himself warm

And hide his head under his wing, poor thing."

"You'd think that is where this nursery rhyme would end. Right little Robin?" Carol asked the baby in her arms. "But my mother didn't like that ending. She said in every life comes winter bleakly, but spring comes and life goes on. So she'd say it like this:

"Bleak in the morning early,

All the hills are covered with snow,

And winters now come fairly.

Wind doth blow and we shall have snow,

And what will poor robin do then, poor thing?

He'll sit in a barn and keep himself warm,

And hide his head under his wing, poor thing.

But winter bides away,

It never seeks to stay,

And robin will peek out his little head,

Life will start anew, as warmth dries the dew,

And the sun will shine again."

"I like that better. Don't you Harriet? I think it means that even though awful things happen and you feel so cold and awful inside that someday it gets better. I know it's getting better for me I hope it's getting better for you but I'll always be there

because were family don't forget that Robin.
I love you little one," Carol exclaimed.

Katha breathed a sigh of relief on hearing
this and smiles thanking Francine silently
for helping Carol. Carol would be okay.
There would still be some tough times ahead
but they could weather them. After all they
were Kelly's not of blood but of heart and
that made them strong.

**The End or is it please read an excerpt
from the next book in the series This
Little Piggy Had None.**

~0~

Excerpt from ~ This Little Piggy Had None

This little piggy went to market

This little piggy stayed home

This little piggy had roast beef

This little piggy had none

And this little piggy went wee wee

All the way home

(Old Nursery Rhyme)

Terrence was extremely excited; tomorrow they would begin construction on the property uptown. The developers would turn into homes for Neddy, his wife, Regan and Carol, of course also homes for Lily, Rose, Amelia, Katha and himself. They would be one happy family with a central room for family events complete with a kitchen and lounge area.

Everyone would have their own huge apartment and everyone would be happy. Was that too much to ask? His family had been through hell. All these murders that had occurred had touched each and every one of them. He could almost believe in a curse but that would mean believing his beloved Katha was cursed and she had never done anything for someone to curse her.

He had been shocked and pleasantly surprised when the old Byers department store building went on the market. The building had been left to decay for the last twenty years so he thought he would get a really good deal but the competition had been fierce; mainly in the form of dealing with that real estate devil, Herbert Weatherthorpe. Weatherthorpe through his lawyer and real estate agent, had tried to undercut Terrence and get the building from Terrence, but Terrence's real estate guru had been better. Now the building was

Terrence's and the construction would soon begin.

Terrence hated that son of a bitch. Terrence felt he had been the ruin of downtown, buying up all the real estate and then renting it out for exorbitant rates or just leaving the buildings to fall apart so he could get around the law and then tear them down because they were now dilapidated and a hazard. Terrence had had to pay more than the building was worth and use a little blackmail to get this building from that swine's grasp. The owner seemed to like Terrence despite that and sold him the building.

Terrence's phone had rang after five p. m.. Terrence had listened intently then had slammed the cell phone down in disgust. The building was supposed to be Terrence's now, but that rotten greedy pig had offered the owner more money.

His real estate agent had called him to tell him the papers had to be signed yesterday, and that Terrence had to come down and fork over another twenty thousand dollars to

the owner to secure the deal. Terrence had
told the real estate man that he would pay no
more. Or that little piggy would find he had
none no reputation, no allies and no money.
Terrence would ruin him. If he thought he
could push Terrence Stewart around the man
could think again. Terrence had been a judge
and he had all kinds of allies both criminal
and law enforcement on his side. That has
settled it all yesterday the building was
irrevocably Terrence's, Weatherthorpe
couldn't touch it now.

Terrence lingered over his coffee nursing his
cup of coffee. He'd better hurry up he had a
breakfast meeting with his old pal, Kerwin
Drake a former defence attorney now
retired. Kerwin had a venture that he wanted
to discuss with Terrence to have him invest
in. Terrence had a few dollars; if the
proposal was sound he could give him a
little money. Then he was supposed to meet
Katha for lunch.

He'd just put his cup in the dishwasher when his cell phone rang. Terrence picked up his cell phone. He thought this better not be the real estate agent asking for yet again more cash. Enough was enough. The deal was signed sealed and delivered it was too late to ask for more.

"Is this Terrence Stewart?" a deep timbered voice asked.

"It is. Who is this?"

"Herbert Weatherthorpe."

So the man dared to call Terrence himself? Ha, Ha, Terrence would have some fun with him. Weatherthorpe could do no harm the building was all Terrence's.

"I see," Terrence answered.

"Don't hang up; we have something to talk about."

"We have nothing to discuss."

"But we do. If you want to truly own the Beyer building…"

"I already own the building," Terrence declared triumphantly.

"Do you have the keys?"

"No," Terrence admitted not knowing quite why he answered that way. He had the key a skeleton key which he picked up at his real estate agent after signing the papers this morning.

"So if you want them meet me at it third floor at precisely eight thirty. Don't be late."

How dare he? Then the cell phone call dropped. Terrence tried to call back the man but no one answered. Should he really satisfy his curiosity and meet the man? Terrence was meeting Kerwin at 8:30 a.m. He didn't have time for this. He'd go to breakfast take his time with Kerwin and he'd then he'd meet the devil at the Beyer building.

Terrence was more than a little annoyed. Why that man had to meet him on the third floor of the Beyer building? Terrence thought in the next moment he wouldn't go! His real estate person had given Terrence the key so why would that bastard Weatherthorpe claim to have keys? Could he have keys?

Yet he was now curious. He had confirmation by fax a few minutes ago, the place was now his. Wouldn't that be fun to wave in that asses face? He'd go if only to do that. Besides that man had no business trespassing in Terrence's building. Katha didn't have to know any of this he hadn't told her anything about Weatherthorpe and his manipulations he didn't need to tell her anything about this now, Terrence wouldn't be late for lunch he'd talk to the idiot; flaunt the deeds in front of Weatherthorpe and then be out of the building by noon to meet Katha.

"Fine I'll come, but that is barely a half an hour from now," Terrence said but he had no intention of being there at eight thirty the fool could wait.

"See you when you get here then," the man cried.

Terrence arrived a little after eleven a.m. and entered through the front door of building with the skeleton key he had picked up at his real estate agent. He then placed the skeleton key in his pocket. Terrence then got on the antique elevator. The elevator creaked and made the usual noises of a decrepit elevator as it went up the floors. Terrence thought maybe he should have taken the stairs. The elevator probably wasn't safe. When had it last been serviced?

The elevator lurched and little then stopped abruptly. Damn it, the elevator had stopped halfway below the floor, Terrence thought. Terrence pulled his body up and out of the elevator and as he did he felt something hard come down on his head and his body pitched forward.

~0~

A short time later as Terrence came to, dazed and confused and looking up into the face of a police officer who stated, "You have the right to remain silent and refuse to answer questions. Do you understand?"

"Where am I?"

"The Beyer building sir. Have you understood your rights as I've told you so far?"

"Rights?"

"Yes, sir," continued the cop, "Anything you do say may be used against you in a court of law. Do you understand? You have the right to consult an attorney before speaking to the police and to have an attorney present during questioning now or in the future. Do you understand? If you cannot afford an attorney, one will be appointed for you before any questioning if you wish. Do you understand? If you decide to answer questions now without an attorney present you will still have the right to stop answering at any time until you talk to an attorney. Do you understand? Knowing and understanding your rights as I have explained them to you, are you willing to answer my questions without an attorney present?"

Terrence held his head trying to understand what was happening. Why was he being arrested? Terrence turned his head and couldn't believe his eyes. Not only was Herbert Weatherthorpe lying close to Terrence with a hammer imbedded in his head; but in Herbert's grasp was a skeleton's hand holding the skeleton key to this building that had been in Terrence's pocket. One finger also pointed pointing to something but what? Terrence tried to pull his thoughts together but he just felt foggy none of this made any sense. Terrence heard another cop came in the room.

"You idiot, Alan! This man is injured he can't understand what you're saying, call an ambulance and get him to the hospital.

Terrence took a deep breath and promptly passed out.

~0~

Excerpt from Stray Bullet

In the small town of Driftwood, Colorado, under starry skies, residents went about their business. The town was now ready for the arrival of the new sheriff having gussied up the urban decay with a few coats of paint. The new sheriff would see the bad parts of town soon enough the mayor thought and turned over in his bed and went to sleep. The hospital looking after a few patients was unusually quiet under the full moon; other people in the settlement getting ready for bed and then turning on late night programs or setting alarms and climbing into bed. Across town a man getting ready for bed after a long hard day at work completed his paperwork, stripped naked and stepped into the shower.

As the water ran down in torrents the shower glass doors shattered, the man fell to the floor and rivets of blood ran into the drain. He was the first to die that night.

A few doors over gunman entered killing the husband and wife in their beds and the children as they slept. Blood covered the floor and ceilings in those rooms. None of the neighbours heard a peep they simply slumbered on. Other homes across the town were entered and the residents, husband wife and children were also shot and killed. No one had time to shout out or call 911. It was all over in a few minutes with no time for whimpers only the muzzle of silencers doing their jobs and hitman scurrying into the night.

"It's done, boss. The teams are leaving the state. Yes, I'll do that now. He's coming in the morning. I'll check in after I meet him. His name? All I got is G. Bullet not sure of his first name, it's not on any paperwork. . See you, tomorrow… okay Friday," the man said into his prepaid cell phone and then took out sim card breaking it into pieces. Then he discarded it in a nearby bin at the now decrepit old pulp and paper mill. He had to go to work soon. A new sheriff was coming to town and he wanted to be there to greet him.

Chapter 1 – Friendship Trumps Bullet

My name is G and I'm on my way to a new life to become a sheriff in a town called Driftwood. Sounds boring, doesn't it. If you'd asked me five year ago I would have told you of course it was; but now this is what I need and my daughter needs…a nice quiet life, in a quiet town, where I could raise my daughter without whispers and rumors. You want to more about that statement? I'll get back to that, but I'm told people will want to know about me a subject I'm not really comfortable talking about.

Asked to describe myself I would say I'm tall over six feet…okay six feet five inches. I am muscular as I lift weights. I'm not overly muscular just enough to take down the bad guys. Some people think I look like Tom Selleck in his youth, personally I don't see the resemblance.

G. is a short form for my first name but I don't like to talk about my real first name. Let's just say my parents grew up in the happy-go-lucky seventies and were heavily influenced by the weird names that people gave their children. What you still won't give up? You demand that I tell you my first name? You want to play the guessing game?

My first name is unmentionable I don't talk about it ever!! My last name is wait for it...Bullet...I know a clichéd name if you ever heard one. Honestly, it's my name. It has been mine my whole life.

My last name had raised a few eyebrows can you imagine how many chuckles I've gotten when I tell anyone my full name? Still can't guess? Some of you have deducted correctly. So now you know why I usually don't divulge my first name.

In order for you to understand the relevance of my last name I'll have to explain more about my family and their origins.

My grandfather when escaping persecution in Russia came through at Ellis Island and decided to Anglicizing his name to Bullet; so my dad used that and now I do. What's that you like to know grandpa's original name? Well so would I, unfortunately he took that name to his grave leaving no clues behind. But he was great man, a hard working cop. I come from a long line of cops. With a last name like Bullet it tends to earn respect being a cop.

Grandpa was killed on the job by some backward gangsters bent on destroying one another. My dad swore he never be a cop and went to San Francisco were he promptly fell in love with my mother went to the police academy there and then impregnated my mother.

After I turned one he decided he needed family and got a job as a cop in the city where his father had served and brothers now served as cops. When he worked there for six months he had planned to send for mom and then marry her.

Unfortunately the first day on the job he ran into a domestic situation and was killed in the line of duty. He hadn't told his family about my mother or me so we came as a surprise when mother showed up with me in tow for the funeral.

When I was four years old, my mother learned she was dying of breast cancer. My dad's three brothers, James, Bennie, and Alfred also cops, stepped up to raise me. They were a demanding bunch always pushing me to be strong and tough. I had to be resilient and learn all the fighting techniques that they taught. Let's say I am proficient in a number of fighting techniques.

Their younger sister, my Aunt Louisa was a teacher and just starting her career when they took me in however Aunt Louise found time for me. She made my childhood more normal though my uncles would often say she shouldn't coddle me. My uncles drove her away with their constant beratement and by the time I was in my teens she moved to teach in Colorado to save her sanity.

She still managed to chide the uncles into letting me visit her in Denver in the summer for two months; the best two months of the year for me.

Getting back to my uncles they hated my first name as much as I did (though I think they liked me even less; but did their duty). They also felt that I had come out of nowhere so they nicknamed me Stray and it stuck; that's what most of the cops on the force called me. Aunt Louise was the only one who ever called me; by my first name.

Aunt Louise had recently retired to a small town called Driftwood Colorado and I wished she had been closer especially when I had run into the wall of blue at my job. Cut to today as I told you earlier I'd taken a new job as the sheriff in Driftwood Colorado.

As I drove to the Sheriff station; I saw that the downtown area was newly painted but other parts were decrepit and rundown. Stores had been closed and signs had been posted that said for rent but the places looked like they hadn't been rented in a long time. The back alleys showed signs, of hookers working their wares with discarded condoms.

The town was surrounded by trees; but the main source of jobs in the past had been lumber and the company had pulled up stakes and moved away. Factories and brickyards were closed. Some of the homes have seen better days and the downtown core was eerily quiet, with vacant storefronts lining the streets. Crime which in the past hadn't been a problem was suddenly up and maybe that's why the Sheriff had quit? But that was the reason I was here. I'd shape this town into a town we could all be proud of again if the re-elected mayor could do as he promised and bring in the jobs. I wanted to be happy here.

I'd just dropped off my three year old daughter with my Aunt Louise. Stella Marie, my daughter seemed okay with the new place and Aunt Louise; but was I? Aunt Louise was sixty years old and a retired school teacher. Why was I so worried? First day jitters obviously. Aunt Louise had my back.

She knew what idiots her brothers really
were and how they valued their friendships
even more than family. Being a single father
I needed her more than ever.

Aunt Louise had urged me to apply for the
vacant job of Sheriff after hearing about my
troubles as a cop in a suburb of Halton,
Illinois. I don't want to get into those
troubles right now. Today was a new day
and I decided it was going to be great even if
it killed me. Just kidding! I was not going to
get killed like my dad had on the first day of
the job. Nerves were getting to me.

Sure it was hard settling into a new place for
a child. A little voice worried that I had
made a mistake; but this was a new start for
both of us we should be happy. A month ago
I had been offered my dream job, Sheriff of
a small municipality in Driftwood,
Colorado. Driftwood looked to me like a
small town of three hundred people where
I'd be happy raising Stella-Marie.

The streets were tree-lined; the cookie cutter houses had beautiful floral displays out front. The lawns were immaculate green and lush. Children rode their bikes up and down the streets with no fear of predators or gunplay. The people had seemed friendly and warm when I came for my interview for the job. What more could we want? I'd thought.

I'd done my research; but nothing had prepared me for the men all walking out on me. I stepped into the Sheriff's car.

This blue flu wouldn't do! I knew from the dispatcher that the other cops were not happy with my appointment; but damn it was my first day on the job and they had a duty to serve and protect the citizens of Driftwood.

How could the four deputies just not show up for the day? Calls to their residences had gone to voice mail so they were even avoiding talking to me. I had to put my foot down hard or the men would never respect my leadership. I'd already faced a wall of blue in my old job; people pulling out the old politics line and drawing in ranks on the thin blue line. I'd wanted a new start to change the harassment I'd faced in my not so fair city over the last three years.

A bit of a long story which we'll get into later but suffice to say the line in blue was put up against me; simply because I stood up to another cop who committed a crime.

Driving down the road to go to my new deputy's home I grew angry. Hadn't I been through enough of this crap from the guys in Halton? I had been harassed day and night by those assholes.

I had to pull myself together, anger would not solve this problem. I could show them I was in charge but approachable. I was an outsider, hired on line. Hell I hadn't even met any of this guys but I would get along with them they just had to give me a chance.

No that sound desperate and I wouldn't be that anxious. I would be the best Sheriff and boss they ever had.

I parked the squad car and mounted the wooden steps on the house. I knocked lightly on Deputy Gregory Barnes door. No answer. I gave it my best thundering police knock and the door swung open of its own accord. I pulled my service revolver and entered the residence wily. A smell of dead berries and apples entered my nostrils. I felt in my pocket and swished my menthol medicated lip balm under my nose. My adrenaline kicked in and suddenly I felt exhilarated and hyper aware.

I followed the putrid odor to a bedroom and found the late Greg Barnes with two bullet wounds to the heart surrounded by a dried rusty brown pool of blood. He'd been there at least two days. Nothing was disturbed in the home. No overturned furniture, nothing seemed out of place. He lived alone; so no help there. Was it a rogue girlfriend? Why was he dead?

What the hell? The first day on the job and my deputy is murdered? I needed those other cops that hadn't come to work today to help me solve this murder. Damn them and their blue flu.

I made the call to the coroner who was on call for autopsies. Then I secured the scene and called in the neighboring counties police force on loan until I could find my police force.

Less than an hour later, I had two officers, Alfred Jones and Paulo Scarlatti, I sent to the two of them to retrieve the first officer Joseph Paciocco on my list. Imagine my surprise when he called back to tell me that my other officer, Joseph Paciocco was dead too. Two shots to the heart and it looked like the same felon. Was I going to find all my missing officers dead?

A quick search of the other residences found all of the bachelor cops dead shot the same way. The family men with their families at home were dead too; but so were all their family members. They had all been shot with one shot to the head in their beds. They had not stood a chance. This was a professional job as each scene had been carefully scanned and nothing was left to find in the way of evidence other than the blood and bullets.

All in all the dead were Gregory Barnes, Joseph Paciocco, Jack Abrahams, Paul Jones, Harold Jones and his wife Cheryl, their two children Gail, and Fred, Vincent Vecchio and his wife Paula Antrim (both cops on the force), their baby, Adrian a newborn was alive in his crib and was taken into custody of the Children's Aid until a relative could be reached. Also dead were Robert Di Salvio and his wife Rebecca and their fifteen year old son William and their daughter Helen eight years old, Kas Mahmoud his wife Dayita, and their three sons, Aaban, Aahil, and Aatif ages five seven and nine.

What in the hell was going on? Someone had killed whole families. Why? Did they know something someone didn't want them to know? Was it retaliation?

This meant looking into backgrounds and finding out things people didn't want you to know. Being sheriff didn't make for a popularity contest in any case but this would have to be handled very delicately.

The police officers on loan couldn't continue to investigate this; I only had a temporary loan of their services for today. Even if I wanted to investigate I had to have help. I needed to call the FBI pronto and I knew just the guy my former partner Gordon Chum.

I dialed Gordon's number by heart. He answered on the first ring asking me about the new job and then said he'd speak to his boss and get the okay to bring a team down as soon as possible.

Meanwhile I was trying to comfort the staff left at station and ducking calls from reporters from all over the country and residents of Driftwood who were demanding to know what had happened. I took deep soothing breaths…Gordon would be here soon we'd get to the bottom of this. Penny Ambercrombie the office dogsbody and police dispatcher took charge and hustled the troops off to their stations to work on the tasks I'd given them.

Penny was tall and lean possibly one hundred and ten pounds though it was hard to tell for her clothes hung on her in nondescript browns that did nothing to enhance her looks and she was well over five feet eleven. Her hair was a rich chestnut and was wound tightly at the nap of her neck into a bun. Her eyes were her most striking feature that not even her terrible clothes sense could hide as they were a glittering emerald green that showed immense interest and intelligence. She appeared to be in her late twenties though her skin was leathered with the weathering an outdoors enthusiast had.

I could see that Penny was an asset to me and the sheriff's station in my job. But first I needed to call Aunt Louise and Stella- Marie and hope my daughter wouldn't get too upset that daddy would not see her until tomorrow at the earliest.

I picked up the phone and called the number by heart. There was no answer. Where could she be I wondered? My question was answered in the next few seconds by my office door swinging open. There my Aunt Louise stood with Stella Marie. Aunt Louise demanded, "Gunnar is it true? Are they all dead?"

The next thing that happened was three year old Stella-Marie jumping in my arms and saying "Daddy, I missed you."

I closed my office door no sense in putting on a show to the remaining troops and I hoped no one had heard my aunt utter my first name. Stella-Marie took the chair nearest me.

"I want an answer Gunnar."

"Not in front of the c.h.i.l.d."

"Ch. i. l.d, child, that's me," my precocious daughter answered.

"Stella-Marie already knows all about this. She turned on the television while I was in the bathroom and she heard about all your deputies and their families being found dead. She insisted I bring her here."

"Then you both know what I know. I'm investigating and I've called in the FBI."

"Daddy, are you safe? In that movie with the Kung Fu guy they tried to kill him and then killed his family," Stella-Marie answered.

"What have you been watching?"

"I remember his name. I love Jean Claude van Damme movies," Stella-Marie stated.

"Me too, pumpkin and we're safe. I haven't been here long enough to be mixed up in whatever is going on here," I reassured.

"You'll find the bad guys?"

"Daddy will find them. That's what daddy used to do before he had you," I answered.

"Be careful," Stella-Marie said with adult wisdom beyond her years.

"Stella-Marie is correct. You need to stay safe."

"I promise both of you, I will stay safe."

"We'll trust you."

"Can we have dinner together, daddy?"

"Of course we can, my apple dumpling.

"I'm not an apple dumpling."

"No, you're my little pumpkin."

"You're silly, daddy."

"What would you like for dinner? Pizza? Chinese food?"

"Pizza. I want pizza!!"Stella-Marie chimed.

I ordered her favourite Hawaiian pizza and we forgot work for a few minutes as we ate. Stella-Marie told me about her day between bites. Stella-Marie sounded happy and adjusting well to living in this new place. She didn't seem too worried about my job anymore. She kissed me goodbye and said, "Get'em, daddy. See you tomorrow, nighty, night."

I breathed a sigh of relief my daughter seemed happy despite all that was happening. I was the new sheriff so the danger to me from who ever committed these murders must be minimal if any, so my family was safe. Still I told Aunt Louise to keep Stella-Marie indoors and keep the doors locked reporting any suspicious activity to me.

Gordon arrived a few minutes later, "I'm Special Agent Gordon Chum FBI," he said showing his badge then continuing he said, "I'm here to take over this case."

"No. You're not you're here to assist me and the good people of Driftwood."

"I am here to serve the people yes and if that means taking over the investigation in a town that has seen fit to kill all its police officers save one..."

"How dare you? This town is peaceable. There is a perpetrator or perpetrators who have committed a heinous crime but we will get to the bottom of this."

"You should have recused yourself Sheriff."

I heard Penny Ambercrombie gasp and then mutter under her breath, "What a maniacal idiot and a kook to boot."

"No, I shouldn't recuse myself!" I replied to Gordon, "This maybe my first day on the job but I am imminently qualified to investigate this. I hadn't even met these men or their families; but I care very much about what has happened to them. They are police officers and my squad. Every one of them is mine so this crime was done against me and my family. Do you understand?"

"I understand the feeling and I promise not to step on your toes, Sheriff. My men and I are at your disposal in this investigation. You are in charge. Perhaps we could discuss the particulars before my colleagues get here?" Gordon stated.

"Please follow me this way to my office, Special Agent Chum," I answered.

"Call me Gordon," my pal offered.

"People call me Stray," I stated.

Gordon pretended to be shocked and lifted an eyebrow at me. Penny looked at Gordon with disgust but went back to the front desk of the station.

Gordon entered my office and shut the door, loudly. Spotting the pizza he said, "That went well."

"Yes, it did. Did you see the dispatcher, Penny Abercrombie craning her head and her ears to listen to you?"

"I saw her when I came into the station. She was frowning at you and giving you dirty looks when you weren't looking like she didn't believe you belonged here."

"I noticed those looks all day," I answered.

"That should be the end of that you can thank me now. She is directing those looks to me now and I'll wager she'll spread all over town how you defended the honor of the dead."

"Thanks Gordon for the assist; but how will we can we keep up the lie?"

"We begin a new friendship," Gordon said calmly then continued, "I hope you saved me a few slices of that I'm starved and my team is checking into the No-Tell Motel down the street within the hour."

I smiled and nodded handing him a couple of slices. It was good to see my old partner again.

"You are staying with me and Aunt Louise aren't you?" I asked.

"Lucky for you or is it me they are limited space in this town to stay and of course this allows me to begin a new friendship with you. All my agents have taken up the last rooms in the motel so I'm grateful your aunt will put me up. You did ask her didn't you?"

"Didn't think I had to. Aunt Louise loves you."

Gordon raised another eyebrow.

"Fine, I'll call her now."

I dialed and Aunt Louise answered her cell phone on the first ring. Aunt Louise said of course Gordon was staying here. I told her not to tell anyone we knew her and she agreed after I told her why. Then she said she had to go as she had pulled over to answer the cell phone.

"So it's settled?" Gordon asked.

I nodded.

"What a terrible first day on the job for you pal," Gordon commented, "Especially after what happened to you more than three and half years ago."

I thought back to what I had been through the last three and half years and I found myself reliving that chaotic time in my mind.

I'd been about eight years on the job in the city of Halton, Illinois, a cop, just like my dad and grandfather and uncles before me. The city had gone to the gangs. . It was two steps and one step forward. Every time we turned around; another shooting another victim of a drive-by. Just the other day the victim was a seven year old kid innocently riding their bike! Luckily the kid lived; but we actively hunted for the shooter or shooters. I should have took that as an omen seeing as my grandfather and my dad lost their lives in the police service, but I went merrily on my way doing my job not expecting my life to come crumbling all around me.

A routine call to a richer neighborhood for a disturbance started it all. The dispatcher didn't think to tell me it was a domestic disturbance and the man had a gun. I'm always careful in those situations; more careful then the average cop but if you don't know you can't take precautions.

I knocked on the door and announced myself and shots barreled through the front door grazing my forehead and tearing my knee apart. I burst through the door grabbed the shooter and he shot me again. That should have got me accolades and medals right? After all I was shot doing my job, but no, all of those rightly went to my partner, Gordon Chum. The third shot resulted in a thigh wound that almost made me bleed out on the spot if it wasn't for the quick work of my partner Gordon Chum securing the prisoner and belting my thigh. Okay, so I got a medal or two, but Gordon was the real hero. See why he was the first man I called when my force had been gunned down.

Gordon is a second generation Asian American. A good looking fellow and kinder than most men, he speaks softly and carries a big stick. People underestimating him rather walk away unscathed. Gordon standing at five foot six weighed roughly two hundred and ten pounds of pure muscle. He knew every fight technique I knew and more. He saved my life a time or two.

Gordon was arguably one of the best partners I've ever had. Gordon saved my life after I was shot on duty and secured the

scene until back-up could get there. He also
called for an ambulance for me. I was carted
off to a hospital where I spent the next three
weeks in intensive car being prayed over by
my fellow cops, and the rest of the city.

Whatever chits they called in with the big
guy upstairs it worked, I survived and I
should have been happy about that; but all I
could think was I missed my moment I was
supposed to die like my dad and my
grandfather before me on the job. It wasn't
that I was that different when I came out of
the coma. Okay, so I had a few scars inside
and out. My forehead now sported a scar
that I could cover with bangs and
temporarily bum leg. The leg didn't seem to
want heal in fact at one point they threatened
to take off my leg; but good old Gordon
helped me fight them on that and the knee
healed to the point I could walk on it. But it
wasn't good enough for work, at least not
then.

Suffering from self-loathing (and yes a little
post-traumatic stress disorder, if I truly
admit it); I began to be curt with everyone

closing myself off from everyone and everything. My wife, Gina took the brunt of all of this. I was cruel to her at every turn. When she came to visit I'd ignore her.

I knew I needed help from the police shrink but I couldn't accept or admit that I, the wonder boy actually had a problem. Gordon begged me to quit loathing myself so much and making everyone else around me miserable but I didn't listen. I was content to wallow in my anger and self-loathing.

Weeks went by and Gina seemed unhappy despite her forced saccharine with me. She gave me an ultimatum get help; or she would leave me. I decided I wanted Gina so I found a shrink of my own choosing Doctor Collins for his add in the Yellow Pages.

Doctor Collins turned out to be a woman. Don't get me wrong she wasn't a fantasy (that blonde fantasy with legs up to here and hiding behind glasses); no she was more like your grandmother. Non-descript, her silver hair short and curled tight to her head. Her voice was soft and she always offered me milk and cookies before a session. I kind of felt weird at first like she was family and I'd never been all that chatty with family anyway. I had so much trouble talking at first that I'd just sit there and stare at the walls; but after a few sessions she got me to open up about my childhood and then finally about the shooting. I began to feel better and worked on getting my knee back in shape so I could return to work.

I had a routine and I followed it. Therapy followed by afternoon sessions of psychotherapy. With the drugs Doctor Collins prescribed and all our talks I began to almost feel normal again. Okay, so I'm lying; I still had a few stray thoughts that I was a failure and that I should have died; but I labored hard to overcome them and worked on being nicer to my ball and chain. I even began to buy her flowers. As for my leg it was almost good enough to return to work.

Doctor Collins had scheduled my appointment for two p.m. on a Friday and I had looked forward to getting it over with and going home to surprise Gina. A cop buddy had offered me his family cottage and I planned a trip to the Poconos for the next week. I'd already called Gina's work and got her the next week off. It would be a fantastic surprise for her and a chance for us to just lay back and enjoy our weekend. I could even cook all the meals that I caught from the lake as it was loaded with fish.

I decided to change my appointment and let Gina know that it would now be at noon instead of two p.m... Surely I could charm my shrink into seeing me earlier and if not well then I see her next week after my trip. I arrived at the doctor's office to find a note on the door. It seemed my shrink. Doctor Teresa Collins had died suddenly this morning and they were rescheduling. A number to call followed the announcement.

Died! And all they thought about was their schedule? Devastating and only then realizing how close I had gotten with my shrink I fell to the floor crying and took about a half- an -hour to recover enough just to pull myself together. I told myself over and over everything would be okay but I didn't really believe it.

Enough of this shit!! A little therapy and I turned into a wimp; who cried at the drop of a hat. I was a Bullet and we were strong manly types; made of steel not mush!! People died!! Get over yourself I admonished myself. I had a life... a wife who loved me despite myself. It was time to man up and be the husband she deserved. I just had to get away with Gina. I'd go home and surprise her now.

Stopping at the gas station to fill-up and walking into pay I spotted roses. I picked some up and thought how pleased Gina would be. She deserved this after all I'd put her through the last two months. She'd surprised me two weeks ago, telling me that she was pregnant. I was overjoyed looking forward to our baby coming in six months. We had a new beginning and I would make her as happy as Gina had made me.

I thought about the look on her face; her joy at our baby and decided to book her favourite restaurant before we left town. We could then leave at nine p.m. I'd drive all night and we reach there by morning. It could be done despite my gimpy leg. Okay so I lied, I wasn't fully recovered; but soon I would be. My physical therapist was pleased and said I might even be able to go back to work in a month.

I went home opening the front door with my key and... You know what happened? It was that other old cliché...husband comes home and finds his wife naked doing the tango with another naked man.

I didn't recognize him from the back as he jumped out the window, naked clothes in hand. She could tell me who he was in her own good time. And I had plenty of time as I seethed and wanted to kill him but not her. I didn't want to hurt her at all I just wanted to take her in my arms and make this go away.

I took huge breaths and then realized it takes two to tango. I had brought this on with neglect and coolness towards her when all she did was support and love me. I took deep breaths to calm myself and rationalized. I was sure this was just a one-time thing.

I'd heard women could get quite horny in pregnancy I obviously had let her down.

I had been a terrible husband moody brooding, distant and angry. Gina deserved better and I could forgive her this. Couldn't I? Sure I was angry, but I would never harm Gina despite my thinking for her lapse in judgement. I had stared at her five foot nine naked figure with its well-endowed breasts and tiny waist and wondered how she hid our baby in it.

Her curly black hair fell in ringlets to her waist. I realized I loved her. I loved our baby. It had been my neglect that had driven her to this; I was prepared to forgive her and take her on my planned trip. We'd been

married fifteen glorious years, okay so not
glorious, fiery but she was also pregnant and
I wanted my child to have a stable home
with two parents one of them me. I'd been
spared so my kid could grow up with a dad
it was as simple as that.

I told Gina all of this and she laughed. It
seems that she and her paramour had been
carrying on since day one of one of our
marriage. Once more she had an
amniocentesis last week and received the
results this morning the baby was his not
mine. I was devastated all those dreams of
playing catch with my daughter. Taking her
to daughter and daddy dances. Having her
look up to me, with hero worship came
crashing down. Yes, I know it could have
been a boy; but I had my heart set on a girl.

I admit it I went against all my principles
and begged her to stay and claim the baby
was mine. We were married so the baby was
legally mine. She laughed that twinkly laugh
that I knew so well and I had to restrain

myself from retaliating as she told me she already left me I just hadn't noticed. Gina said she was tired of living a lie. Now that I knew it was all out in the open and she file for divorce and move in with him. She lunged at me slapping me and asked why could I be like him?

I want to hit back at her but I couldn't if I it back I wouldn't be any better than the men I arrested who abused their wives.

Why couldn't I be like him? The man that she slept with she raged at me. I was stupefied and getting angrier by the moment I knew I needed to leave before I regretted losing my temper; but I needed to know who had replaced me.

She laughed again and said I find out soon. I begged her to tell me and she did.

HIM? I fell to my knees. How could it be him? No, it wasn't Gordon Chum; but someone else I considered a friend and brother. Gordon wouldn't do that to me. The dirty dog who had betrayed me had been a partner, a mentor and good grief the man was old...fifty five if he was a day and close to retirement.

Why had she cheated on me with my former partner Derek? He'd broken the cop code you didn't sleep with another cop's wife. He'd slept around I heard how many women he'd been with had she? I told her and she laughed telling me it was his cover story. She continued snickering and said at least every woman didn't try to pick him up in front of her. She packed her bags and then trounced out the front door to join him at his house.

I thought I could handle it all and maybe I could have if she hadn't come back a half an hour later saying she'd changed her mind. She stripped to her skivvies and begged me to change her mind. What's a hot blooded male to do? I wanted to prove I was the better man, the better lover, so I turned my back and began stripping too.

That's the last thing I remember before waking up in hospital. How I got there and what happened after that I couldn't recall until much later.

The doctor kept speaking to me but it sounded like gibberish. My brain didn't want to understand. I don't know why. I closed my eyes, but before I drift under I hear them talking.

"Will he be okay now, doctor?" Gina asked.

"We'll know better when he answers my questions," I perceive the doctor say far away.

I heard footsteps as someone left.

A voice I recognize as Gina whispered in my ear, "You stupid son of a bitch. Why didn't you die? You'll wish you had now."

I struggle to wake before she can harm me but it's like moving under quicksand. I hear an alarm sound and footsteps run into the room.

"What did you do you now, you evil bitch?" I heard Gordon yell as I feel myself falling through layers of unconsciousness into nothingness.

~0~

Excerpt from Dreams Can Kill

Chapter 1- Survival

T he rain pelted down on me, as I

struggled to come to my senses. My head felt like it had split in two, as if little lumberjacks had taken up residence. I opened one eye. The world spun sideways like a ride at the fair. I tried shutting one eye, then the other. I nearly fell back to sleep. I opened my eyes again, fighting the sleep which wanted to overtake me. I shuttered my eyes again, as my stomach protested. My whole body manipulated, bruised, bent and broken like some old rag doll discarded.

Sleep...sleep would solve my problems, my brain protested. No! I had a reason I needed

What Will Poor Robin Do?

to stay awake and alert...A little sleep, a part of me protested again. No, I must stay conscious. But I remained so tired. I dragged myself across the pebbled ground. My right leg stuck out at an impossible angle, obviously broken. I saw by lifting my head slightly and turning it that there appeared to be a road up ahead. I had to get to the road. If I dragged myself that far, surely I would be rescued?

But it was oh so hard, to drag yourself backwards, when you couldn't perceive where you were going. Oh no, what if he came back. He would finish me off...finish what he had started.

He who? Who was this person, who left me to die? Why couldn't I remember? Don't panic... the thing to do is right now is to reach help; then and only then would I be safe. I caressed large pieces of gravel which cut into the back of my head. I sensed I was close to the road. I reached out with my good hand and touched a paved surface. I knew I didn't have much strength left. I experienced the energy drain quickly leaving my body. I tried to fight the drain, but the world faded to black.

Chapter 2- Time Flies When You're Having Fun

I opened my eyes slowly. A tube appeared to have been inserted in my arm, feeding me intravenously, another tube down my throat as well. The lumberjacks in my head had been replaced by a dull achy sensation, as if I wasn't quite there. I suffered from weakness all over, but my body didn't have the same sensation, as when I had blacked out on the road. My leg felt whole again and yet my leg didn't appear to be in a cast, or slung up on a tripod. How much time had passed? This definitely looked like a hospital room. The walls were pale white and I lay in a single bed. I rested in a private room how about that?

A nurse in a white cap entered the room. She grabbed my wrist and she proceeded to take my pulse. Alarmed, she stared straight into my face, "Well! Look who is awake.

Welcome back to the real world," she proclaimed.

I tried to speak and realized the tube in my throat prevented that. Why was a tube in my throat I wondered? How long I been here? I assumed I looked scared because the nurse explained in a soft voice, "There, there honey, you take deep breaths, easy now."

"Why don't I go get the doctor? He can come and have a look at you and remove the tube from your throat."

I tried to nod my head in agreement but my head moved like lead. It seemed like eons before a man in a white doctor's coat appeared at my bedside. He appeared tall and lanky; with dark curly brown hair and warm deep blue eyes. Without any preamble he announced, "We will now remove this tube. Take a big breath now."

The tube came out as I gagged. Now I could ask the questions which plagued me.

"How did I get here? And where am I?" I tried to ask, croaking out the words, as if my voice hadn't been used in a while.

"Speak slowly. Here, have sips of water," answered the doctor.

"How did I get here?" I repeated, sure that I had been speaking clearer because I had taken a sip of water.

"I don't know who found you, but an ambulance brought you here in critical condition. You had a broken leg, some broken ribs, and a fractured skull."

"I came here in critical condition? So I've been here awhile?" I asked shocked.

"Yes, you've been here awhile. You were at a different hospital first. You are in Andrews' clinic now."

"Your condition appeared to be perilous there for some time. They lost you twice. We had placed you in a coma to let your brain swelling go away. Then we didn't know if you would ever come out of the coma."

He continued to explain like he couldn't quite find the words. But why would a doctor have trouble explaining a medical condition?

"I guess time flies when you have fun," I stated flippantly, hiding fear I didn't quite understand and becoming puzzled.

Why did he say first they then we? Hadn't he been there?

"I would like to examine you to see how you're doing now and get an update on your condition."

"I'm good. As you can see," I answered in response.

"I don't know if you even realize, but your speech isn't as clear as you think. You're slurring your words," he stated. "I'm sure the words will come easier in time, but I'd like to check your reaction time and some other physical reactions."

What could he be talking about? I wasn't slurring my words. Was I?

The doctor began his examination. A flashlight flashed deep into my eyes. I blinked in response, as the light, so bright, made my eyes hurt. His response seemed to be to write down something on the chart, and pick up my wrist to take my pulse and blood pressure. He then listened to my chest with his stethoscope.

I moved my head and tried to sit up, but the effort zapped all my remaining strength. I surprised myself at how I felt like a newborn baby. He continued his examination. I grew tired but fought the sensation. If I closed my eyes for a moment, would the feeling would go away? I closed my eyelids and fell fast asleep.

What Will Poor Robin Do?

I ran over hills. The night appeared so dark, and ink black; I could barely view two feet in front of me. My feet stumbled, as I tried to see the uneven ground in front of me. My palms clenched with sweat, as my heart pounded like the organ would jump out of my chest. I turned around, my eyes darting from side to side searching for my pursuer. No sign, but I knew he wasn't far behind.

My hair in a high ponytail, whipped at my face, as I picked up the pace in my flight. He seemed close enough, that I had the sensation of his breath on my neck… so close he might reach out and touch me. I turned again to see if I could glimpse him near, and I saw a man. But what puzzled me was what materialized in the man's face. Where his face should be, a gaping black hole yawned.

How could this be? The thought plagued me only for moment, as fear gripped me and survival instinct kicked in. Realizing if he caught me I would be killed, I ran stumbling over rock and uneven ground. When the inevitable happened, I tripped falling to my knees. He had me. There was no escape

from my fate. I would die now. I struggled
as he grabbed my left wrist twisting my arm.

This appeared no dream, I might awake
from; he had me now and he would kill me.

I twisted slightly trying to free my wrist but
he grabbed my other wrist and shook me
slightly saying…, "Quite a dream you were
having, but a dream none the less. Nothing
can harm you now."

I stared into his face and slowly his look
changed, from the faceless man, to another
face entirely. This wasn't the man in my
visions; the demon in my nightmare. I knew
in my heart this remained an altogether
different kind of man.

This face with smiling blue eyes radiated
warmth, and kindness. His face stayed
gentle, not violent. I had been dreaming and
had mistaken his touch for the man in my
dreams. I flushed with embarrassment.

"You are quite awake now? I won't harm you. Now, do remember me?"

I stared at him, slowly waking up, and realizing where I was.

"I'm your Doctor, Doctor Andrews, at your service, my lady. We met before when you awoke from your coma," he continued speaking softly, and gently, bowing at the waist and smiling.

Shouldn't I have recognized him immediately? Heat rushed to my cheeks, as I turned red in embarrassment.

I was a fish out of water. I didn't like the way I reacted; like something had happened and all was a secret to me. I liked to be in charge of my life every aspect, and right now it seemed like I appeared in charge of nothing.

"How long have I been here?" I whispered, trying to speak louder.

"I would have said it's a lot longer, than you think," he replied cryptically.

"Do you always answer a question with a question? I want an answer for my query," I demanded angrily.

"What do you remember?"

"I believe I asked you to stop making this an interrogation. If you must know, I remember waking up a little while ago the nurse came in and then you came a little later," I answered exasperated, wondering what could be wrong with me. I didn't get angry so easily. Did I? Why did I behave this way? Everything he said seemed to make me angry.

"Your little while ago was two days ago...," he explained, breaking off as if afraid to say more.

"But that's impossible..."

"You fell into a restorative sleep. It is not uncommon for patients who have been in a coma to do so."

"Two days? I slept for two days?" I commented incredulously.

"Yes," Doctor. Andrews stated.

"How long was I in a coma?" I asked worried to hear what he might say.

"What month do you remember?"

"You have to be in charge, don't you? Questions! Questions!" I replied, delaying the answer. I was suddenly afraid that I'd been in this coma far longer than I realized, and grew angrier.

"I know you're scared. Are you sure you want to know? The information can wait," he insisted.

"I'm not scared," I lied with false bravado, "I remember quite clearly the month is March."

"It is the eleventh of September nineteen hundred and seventy-one. Do you remember

what happened the day of the accident?" he
asked.

"That's not possible. I can't have been in a
coma for six months. Why do you lie to
me?" I spat at him.

"I know it's hard to assimilate but time has
passed and it is September," he insisted
softly, but firmly.

"Why do you persist in a lie? What do you
have to gain with this preposterous story?" I
demanded; still not ready to believe this.

"Exactly what do I have to gain? Sharron,
I'm not lying to you," he stated sadly.

Until that moment I hadn't given any
thought to my name, but as Doctor Andrews
called me Sharron, I realized I wasn't even
sure if that was my name. I didn't have a
clue what my name was. My name might be
Sharron, but I didn't recall the name. My
name could be Mary, or Angela, or any
other name in the world. If I had a surname,
I couldn't remember it either. A huge blank
spot stood where any recollection should be.

What Will Poor Robin Do?

How could my last memory be of March,
but I still had no recollection of my name, er
names? This was normal after a long coma. I
decided.

Perhaps my memory had been so underused,
and only had temporary gaps? Or I was
hungry? Yes, it had to be one of those
things. A temporary aberration of the mind...
No need for me to worry. No, need to share
any such information.

My memory was only hiatus. That had to be
the answer. Give it a few days and my
memory would all come back. There was no
need to tell the doctor, especially since my
recollections would all come back.
Absolutely not, I reasoned.

After all what good would it do to tell him?
He'd look at me either with sympathy, or
call in a shrink. I wanted none of the
sympathy, and whispered glances which
would follow. So I had a few memory gaps,
nothing to worry about. It was perfectly
normal after a coma, I reassured myself.

"What will you do with all this information Sharron?" asked Doctor Andrews suddenly concerned.

"I must admit the information was a bit of a shock to find the month was September and not March, but I'm over the surprise. "I'm hungry what does it take to get food around here?'' I demanded, quickly changing the subject. Besides I was ravenous.

"I think you can start some light foods, some soft foods, Jell-O soup etc.," Doctor Andrews spouted. Turning to the nurse he commanded, "Nurse get a light meal for my patient."

"Certainly Doctor," the nurse replied, coming into the room rather quickly, at his summons.

Just when I thought I had successfully gotten rid of the doctor, he turned around and said... "I know you are rather tired and hungry right now, but I'm sure you to want to discuss these revelations later today."

What Will Poor Robin Do?

How could I get him to change his track? I
didn't want to discuss my memory loss with
anyone. I wasn't ready for anyone to find
out I didn't know who I was. If I told him,
would he treat me like a mental patient?

No, I wasn't going to tell him, or anyone. I
needed to fake what I remembered. They'd
never know, I couldn't remember. I would
then have the time to accept this myself, and
hopefully everything would come back. No
one would ever have to know.

Wait a minute, did he know, I didn't
remember? He talked about the fact I'd been
in a coma, but had he given me any knowing
glances? I gave him a sideways glance.
Deciding he didn't have a clue about my
memory problem. I plotted to keep it that
way.

"There is not a lot to talk about; but if you
want to we can discuss my medical
condition we can get to that later," I replied,

hoping he would take my response as an agreement and leave.

Luckily for me he took the hint. Maybe he would even forget to come back and discuss this later? No, I hoped for too much, but he did look convinced that I'd talk to him later. Good then he'd go away.

"I will return later, Sharron."

He then left taking his questions with him. I breathed a sigh of relief. Now alone with my thoughts, surely I'd conjure up a memory or two. First I would eat and refuel. That would help the memories, as well as my stomach.

I stared at the food the nurse had brought in. I'm starving to death and the nurse gave me not enough food to feed a rabbit? I tried to pick up the spoon and found my hand wouldn't cooperate.

"Would you like some help?" the nurse asked kindly.

"I can do it myself," I responded stubbornly.

Although I had found it difficult to raise my hand to my mouth, that soon became easier. I found by clamping my hand around the spoon I could manage to feed myself. It was then I realized how much work I had ahead of me. The nurse watched, so I smiled at her like everything was fine. She smiled back and left.

I soon made short work of the food and wanted to move on to the therapy I recognized I needed. I would set the memories, or lack of them aside, and working on building up the muscle tone and abilities I'd lost. When the body restored itself, I would begin to remember. I understood without being told, that I had to begin like a baby to exercise my limbs and I wanted to start immediately. Let's be honest. I realized I could remember something. I grasped now that I was an impatient person, at least when it came to doing things I had to be doing. I called the nurse on the call bell to ask about therapy and exercises.

"Yes?" I heard a disembodied voice somewhere over my head say. Momentarily puzzled, I then realized the voice came from an intercom.

"Sorry to bother you but when can I start therapy? I need to get my limbs moving," I explained.

"Dear, you are barely out of coma. I'm sure your doctor would want you to build up your energy first. Or wait at least until you started solid foods."

She sounded surprised and had a hint of censor in her voice. No support there. I wanted those six months back, but clearly that wasn't going to happen. Move on, I told myself. I'd wasted six months sleeping, time to fight back and get back into fighting form as they said. But who had said that?

I somehow knew I was a fighter. I'd have to
do everything myself; something I knew I
always did. But how did I know that?

I thought about what would work, and what
limbs need to work. My hands needed to a
work out. Okay, they need to grip. How do
you make hands stronger?

You give them something to grip. Squeezing
something soft, medium soft, would work.
Where to get something to work my grasp? I
couldn't even get out of bed. My limbs were
useless, absolutely useless. My hand shook
in weakness, from forcing the stupid thing,
to do its job and feed me.

All of this began to feel hopeless. ..No, I
wasn't some stupid helpless female. I had to
figure out a plan. You're on your own, I told
myself, nothing new. You can overcome any
odds. Think, Sharron, think!

How about some finger exercises? Slowly working each finger, and then in tandem, I would get back movement. I began the exercise I devised. It sounded so simple when I had thought of how to exercise the hand, but painful and tiring. Work through the pain, I told myself. Isn't that what you've always heard?

I forced myself to do the exercises for what seemed like hours, until I couldn't take the pain any more. Then I decided to exercise my arms. Gripping well enough to pull myself up to the bar over my bed, I reached I'm with my right hand to grab the pole. My fingers won't cooperate. My fingers are weakened and my grip slipped. Damn it! Even simple exercise was impossible.

"Nothing is impossible," a voice spoke loudly in my head. But whose voice did I hear? My memory had fled, if it was ever there. I only comprehended the voice had been someone I loved, and respected. Was this a father, or a father figure? I knew I was bone weary, and a great sea of lethargy stole over me. It would be counterproductive not to take a nap, I reasoned. Surely a short nap would restore my energy and I would begin again.

I closed my eyes soon I began dreaming. At first the dream appeared happy. I viewed myself in a beautiful home and grinning at someone I couldn't see.

I smiled and felt great joy, but the sky grew dark and I found myself outside on a field. The moon overhead slowly covered by clouds, and I grew terrified. Something was wrong. The faceless man chased me once more. I ran over rocks and streams and more rocks. He kept coming and coming. I knew he'd soon be on me. He nearly had me when I willed myself to wake up saying… This is a dream and I want to wake up now.

I awoke gasping for air like I had been running a marathon. A strange man sat by my bed. His hair appeared dark, practically black, greasy, and slicked back. He had black thick glasses that he peered over like they were a prop.

An oversized suit coat in plaid and matching pants completed the picture. Despite his harmless appearance, he struck terror to my heart. What gave me the idea he put on this persona, like a piece of new clothing? I think it was his face which seemed to give it all away, like he tried too hard to portray someone he wasn't.

As I gazed at him, he jumped from the chair he sat and exclaimed…"About damn time you woke up out of the coma Sharron. I thought you laze there forever."

He then continued, as if choosing his words carefully, "Oh Sharron, this is the most wonderful day of my life." Then he pulled me to him, fiercely.

"Let go of me, this instance. Who do you think you are? I said don't touch me! And quit acting and looking around there's no audience for your play," I blurted out, before I stop myself.

"Sharron that's not funny. Quit joking. You always had a wicked sense of humour, but

I'm not laughing." the man stated, sounding annoyed and grabbing my wrist.

"I said let me go, and I meant every word. Now kindly take your hands off me," I demanded at the top of my lungs, struggling unsuccessfully to free myself of the grip, he now had on my wrist.

Taken back by my yelling, he let me go, but he still continued to treat me, like a bug under a microscope. Suddenly switching gears, his face changed. It was if a curtain went down over his face. He took on a concerned look and then a hurt look. I admit he nearly had me fooled.

I started thinking I had forgotten a boyfriend, but surely I wouldn't suffer from such bad taste.

He wasn't my type. He seemed quite violent too. I wouldn't have been so foolish to get mixed up with a weirdo like him! Would I?

"Sharron quit staring at me that way you're making me uncomfortable. I'm not amused here...Wait a minute you're not kidding .You don't recognize me at all. You don't recognize your fiancé?"

I recognized somehow that he was put on an act. No, I wasn't engaged to him. If I had been it would boggle my mind. He had to be lying, I decided. Why I didn't know, but I knew he lied.

I had no sparks with him. In fact something about him gave me the creeps. He repulsed me and made my stomach hurt. He certainly didn't sound sincere. He put on an act ... but why? He grabbed my wrists again, once again in a vice grip. I struggled valiantly, but his grip tightened and I couldn't handle his fierce clutch in my weakened stated.

"Let me go you, caveman. I don't know you and what is more, I don't ever want to know you," screamed at him fighting frantically.

"Sharron you cut me to the quick. Why do you say such things to me?" he whined, letting go of my wrist, but gripping my arms even tighter.

Maybe it was because of my dream, but suddenly I was terrified. Why did they leave me all alone with this crazy man? Where was everyone else? Couldn't they hear me shouting?

"Let me go. Let me go....Don't touch me," I yelled at the top of my lungs, and then screamed, hysterically "Help me someone help me."

As I started to pull harder frantically to be free he stilled held fast. What kind of evil demon had me in his grasp? I tried to bite him, but that was impossible; finally in the answer to my screams were footsteps running. Seconds later a nurse and Doctor Andrews entered.

"Let my patient go immediately. I said let her go," Doctor Andrews growled, pulling the man's arms behind his back.

I breathed a sigh of relief. I was safe. Doctor Andrews had saved me.

"I wasn't hurting her! What kind of a man do you think I am? Gee, I have more bruises than her. She acted crazy, so I grabbed both her arms to calm her," the man explained, sounding plausible.

Surely Doctor Andrews and the nurse who followed him in, didn't believe his act?

"Your technique doesn't seem to have calmed her, but it certainly frightened her," Doctor Andrews said, checking my blood pressure and heart rate.

What Will Poor Robin Do?

"You can't tell me what to do. She's my fiancée I can speak to her anyway I want," complained the man, loudly.

"You've upset my patient. Her blood pressure and heart rate is elevated as well. This is not good for my patient, so I can tell you what to do. What is your name?" demanded Doctor Andrews.

"Titus Brown is my name and Sharron is my fiancée," the man replied a little too quickly.

Doctor Andrews consulted his clipboard. He pointed to it and then announced, "This is the approved register and you're not on the list. Leave now, Mr. Brown, or I'll have security escort you out of the facility."

"I'm not going anywhere. Who do you think you are?"

Mr. Brown showed his true colours, I thought. They would trounce him faster than you could say Jack Robinson.

"Mr. Brown, so far I've been pleasant. The nurse has already called for a security guard.

I suggest you leave now and don't come back, or you will find yourself with a trespassing charge and jail time," Doctor Andrews said through his teeth.

"I'll be back with my lawyer and you'll be sorry," Mr. Brown menaced.

Two security guards entered and forcefully removed Mr. Brown from my room. I began to shake like a leaf. I tried to stop, but I grew frightened. Someone had tried to kill me and that is why I was in the hospital. What if it was Him, Mr. Brown?

They wouldn't let him take me when he talked to his lawyer? Would they? Words I hadn't want to share, spilled out of my mouth, first in torments, and then at a screeching level.

"I don't know who the heck he is, but I do know I don't know him. I'm not his fiancée. Don't let him come back lawyer, or no lawyer. I don't want to see him. Someone did this to me! I wouldn't be surprised if the person was him!" I guess I appeared a little too hysterically and forcefully, because the next thing that occurred was Doctor Andrews plunged a needle into me.

"Please, please don't. It's not necessary, really. I'll be good," I pleaded too late.

"It's a little sedative. I don't like your colour, your blood pressure, or your heart rate. You've had a nasty scare and your body isn't able to cope with this right now. Calm down now," he said comforting "Go to sleep."

"I think I hate you," I replied vehemently.

"That's okay, you can hate me if you need to," he answered, smiling.

Damn him and his handsome smile! Something about the grin, made me want to smile back and tell him all my secrets.

"Don't leave me alone. He might come back," I pleaded as I drifted into a deep drugged sleep.

If you enjoyed What Will Poor Robin Do?
Please consider leaving me a few words at
your favourite retailer and if you liked the
excerpts and would like to read more of my
books please check out one of my other
books listed on the next page at Amazon

Sincerely S. G. Lee.

~0~

List of Books by S. G. Lee

Murder Mysteries

Love's Labour's Won

A Tiger's Heart Wrapped in a Player's Hide

Reborn – a novella~ prequel

A Penny Saved A Murder Earned

A Diller A Dollar A Really Dead Scholar

Betty Blue Lost Her Holiday Shoe

What Will Poor Robin Do?

The Kelly Murder Mysteries-Book 1-3

A Stitch in Time

Stray Bullet

Dreams Can Kill

Short Story Books

 Murder Most Fowl

Jack be Nimble

Day of the Dead

Legends, Folktales and other Stories

The Stuff of Nightmares

ObsessionX2

Christmas

Christmas is Calling

The Christmas Card

The Christmas Angel

Visions of Sugarplums

Poetry

A Poetic Touch - The Human Condition

~0~

What Will Poor Robin Do?

408
What Will Poor Robin Do?

www.ingramcontent.com/pod-product-compliance
Lightning Source LLC
Chambersburg PA
CBHW051438260626
47162CB00001B/148